I'M
COMING

I'M COMING

Selma Lønning Aarø

Translated from the Norwegian
by Kari Dickson

ANANSI
INTERNATIONAL

First published in Norway in 2013 by Flamme Forlag
This edition published in Canada in 2015 by House of Anansi Press Inc.

House of Anansi Press
110 Spadina Avenue, Suite 801
Toronto, ON, M5V 2K4
Tel. 416-363-4343
Fax 416-363-1017
www.houseofanansi.com

House of Anansi Press is committed to protecting our natural environment.
As part of our efforts, the interior of this book is printed on paper that contains
100% post-consumer recycled fibres, is acid-free, and is processed chlorine-free.

19 18 17 16 15   1 2 3 4 5

Library and Archives Canada Cataloguing in Publication
Aarø, Selma Lønning, 1972–
[Jeg kommer snart. English]
I'm coming / Selma Lønning Aarø; translated by Kari Dickson.

Translation of: Jeg kommer snart.
Issued in print and electronic formats.
ISBN: 978-1-77089-984-1 (pbk.). ISBN: 978-1-77089-985-8 (html).

I. Dickson, Kari, translator II. Title. III. Title: Jeg kommer
snart. English.

PT8951.1.A564J4413 2015   839.82'374   C2015-901615-0
C2015-901616-9

Library of Congress Control Number: 2015944832

Cover design: Kathryn Macnaughton
Type design and typesetting: Alysia Shewchuk

*We acknowledge for their financial support of our publishing program
the Canada Council for the Arts, the Ontario Arts Council, and the Government of
Canada through the Canada Book Fund.*

Printed and bound in Canada

Are we sick if we don't want sex every day? Every week?
— Toril Moi in *Dagens Næringsliv*, June 1, 2013

Betty: *I was faking.*

Dr. Masters: *You didn't have an orgasm?*

Betty: *You're serious now?*

Dr. Masters: *Yes, I'm serious. You pretended to have an orgasm? Is that a common practice among prostitutes?*

Betty: *It's a common practice amongst everyone with a twat! Almost all women fake orgasms.*

Dr. Masters: *But why? Why would a woman lie about something like that?*

— *Masters of Sex*

MR. R

For a long time, my husband thought I was a horny bitch.

That I came every time we had sex. And that's because I wanted him to think I did. When I was younger, I barely gave any thought as to why I might want him to think that way. I just faked my orgasms, arching my body and moaning, my breathing shallow and frantic. Faking it had to be one advantage of being a woman. At least, that's what I thought for a long time: what a man has to do, a woman can just pretend.

One day I got fed up with faking. Or maybe that wasn't it per se. Maybe I just wanted to feel what he experienced. The great ecstasy. The primal roar. Where did it come from? What did that ecstasy feel like?

When I told A, he was crushed. That's how good I'd been at faking.

At first he thought it was him. Of course he did. He probably thought he wasn't man enough.

It just fell out of my mouth one Friday night. We weren't doing anything in particular. The children were in bed. A was being very compliant. He cleared the table before I had to ask; he stroked my hair and said that he liked my new haircut.

It had been four days since I'd gone to the hairdresser.

Before I knew it, it just popped out of my mouth: "I've never had an orgasm!"

And the first thing he had to be reassured of was that there was nothing wrong with *him*.

I told him that there wasn't, but how could I be sure? It could very well be that he was the problem!

We seldom try anything new. The sequence of our sexual encounters is generally the same. A slips his hand into my panties; he presses his index finger against my clitoris, a little too hard. I moan.

"Yes," I whisper.

He slides into me, thrusts back and forth, massages my breasts without paying much attention to them; he acts as though he is following a manual, as though it's something that I expect.

I lie there thinking about the clothes that have been in the washing machine for an hour. Someone has to hang them up.

He always does the same things. He thinks I like it that way.

I can't blame him. For years I've *pretended* that I like

it. For years I've breathed heavy encouragement in his ear and said yes in a throaty voice. I think that *he* wants it that way. I think that my yeses turn him on, and give him the green light, but maybe they don't. Maybe my moaning and yeses are just as unnecessary for him as the slightly too hard pressure on my clitoris is for me.

The whole thing is usually over and done with fairly quickly. I go to the bathroom to pee. I hang up the clothes or tidy the kitchen.

Sometimes I don't moan as much, which might make him think that he needs to persevere for my sake, even though it's not necessary. I won't come. I can't come.

We refer to it as "the act itself." So really, it's like a play, and we are the actors trying to pretend to satisfy each other.

But A is not the only one to blame for the fact that I don't come. My body is also *my* problem. I can't relax; I'm not thin enough. I don't look like the women in films or in magazines. This is how teenage girls think. But I'm a mature woman, I should have more confidence in myself—I should know better. The older I get, the more distant I become from what they call "the media-made ideal woman." The women in magazines look like they come from a different planet than me; they look like they belong to another race. If female actresses were dogs, they would be greyhounds and I would be a St. Bernard (or possibly, on a good day, a Rottweiler) that's had a bit too much to drink. (I once had a dog, but I'll come back to that later.)

A tells me it doesn't matter. He can say that I'm beautiful — gorgeous, even — but of course I don't believe him. I think he says nice things like that because he wants sex.

I'm always watching myself from the outside, thinking that if our relationship were a film, what kind of film would it be? It's an author's bad habit to constantly reimagine and question oneself — to set a scene. I think any film about A and me would have to be a comedy: all the fumbling, the flaws and failings of our bodies, the unflattering and revealing glare of the overhead light on the bathroom ceiling (we often end up there because it's the only door we can lock without anyone wondering why). The constant need to see myself from the outside means that I don't relax, and someone who can't relax can't have orgasms.

At least, that's the theory I'm working with. So what would happen if I was completely alone, without any witnesses? Would I be able to relax more and envision anything at all? Can't I just close my eyes and be whatever I want? A greyhound? A woman who comes?

I don't think I could ever be someone who just lets go. Every time A comes, I wonder whether the neighbour can hear him shouting. I wonder where the mess is going to end up.

He doesn't think about that. When he loses himself, I can't help but point it out. I might say, "That was a bit unnecessary," if he gets semen on a bathrobe or on the duvet that was changed only a couple of days ago. I'm the sort of person who thinks, "No thanks, I've just had a shower."

I am, quite simply, too practical.

Maybe that's what the problem is? I'm so practical that I can't let go. I'm too practical to have an orgasm.

Mom was incredibly beautiful when she was young, though in a rather standoffish way. I'm not like her: I don't have her long, slender legs, her curls or ice blue eyes. I don't know whether she's had orgasms. She never talked about sex when I was young. She automatically said "oh really" when the word cropped up, but I was okay with that. I had no desire to talk to my mother about sex. I wouldn't have wanted her to be one of those liberal mothers who took me to the doctor and got me a prescription for the pill the first time I made out with a boy. I sorted all that out myself, and my daughters will have to sort it out for themselves, too.

I dread the discussions we'll have to have the day they get their periods. I thought it was so embarrassing to get my period when I was thirteen. I was camping with my dad and brother and I didn't say anything to either of them. As I mentioned, I've always been practical, so I made my own tampon from a bunch of cotton balls, and didn't even consider the risk of infection. When I got home, I was washing my bloody underwear by hand in the bathroom when Mom came in behind me.

"Are you washing your clothes by hand?" she asked. I nodded. "But I could do it in the machine!"

"Mom, I've started my period!" I burst out.

And Mom laughed! She laughed at me! That beautiful face, which I have not inherited, laughed at me. I've never forgiven her.

Mom is the kind of woman who wears an apron in the kitchen. The kind of apron that, when you're five, you can lean your head against or dry your tears and wipe your nose on, and that smells of spices and fried food. Until that day, I thought of that apron whenever I thought of Mom. Those kinds of aprons still remind me of her. But I stopped leaning against her apron after I got my period.

I refuse to believe that I'm frigid. I have feelings. I am horny! That's to say, I *can* be turned on — sometimes. Perhaps not as often as I should, but then again I've been married for a long time. I've given birth to three children and I've nursed them for years. Can you have an orgasm after that?

Apparently you can. Everyone I know gets orgasms. Or at least they say they do. I have a strong feeling that it could happen to me too if I'm just patient enough. I don't want to be *too* horny, of course, just suitably

horny. And I want to have an orgasm. Is that too much
to ask?

A QUICK SUMMARY might be in order. The reasons for
my lack of success in this area to date:

1. I have physical inhibitions.
2. I am too practical.
3. I have a mother.

   Up until recently, I could have also added that I have
too much housework to be able to come, but we've got
an au pair now. And I wouldn't be surprised if that's also
one of the reasons that I can't come. The au pair, that is.
   The house has always been mine: the hectic mornings
in the kitchen, the peace once everyone has left, the piles
of dishes, the overflowing kitchen cupboards — it's mine,
all of it. For ages, A has maintained that I loved to say
that I sacrificed myself for the family, that I played the
victim, emphasizing that I was the only one who ever did
anything in the house. Maybe he's right. Maybe it's something I need to survive: a moral high ground in relation
to him and the kids. I want to feel that I'm indispensible,
that nothing would function without me, that I would
be missed, deeply, if I were to disappear one day. A said
that was why I didn't want a cleaner.

I denied it. I said the whole business of tidying up before the cleaner arrived was just as much work as doing the actual cleaning. And what would I do with myself while this person was cleaning? Would I have to leave my home office and wander the streets for four hours? Or even worse: would I have to sit and watch another person, who was less fortunate than me, wash away all my family's dirt while I just pretend that it isn't happening?

None of the alternatives were attractive.

So we've never had a cleaner. I've washed all the floors, folded all our clothes, and made all our food myself. Until six months ago.

A was adamant that not having a cleaner was something *I* wanted, and as long as it was what *I* wanted, I couldn't count on any help from him or anyone else in the household. When I was actually writing books, there may have been reason to have a cleaner, but it's been a while now since I wrote anything. My poetic rapture is definitely a thing of the past. Writing was easy to begin with when there were practically no obstacles. Things fell into place when I sat down to write. There were almost too many ideas. But then it stopped. It's impossible to generate anything from my life at the moment.

I've always used other people's lives, and now that doesn't work either. I can't seem to give a voice to anything outside myself. It feels false.

Of all the stuff I've written, I like the book I wrote

about my great-aunt and great-uncle best. She had a relationship with a German soldier during World War II and was also sent to a prison camp. My great uncle, who was a student, was arrested and sent to Germany in 1942. Their mother, my great-grandmother, took ill as a result, which probably affected my great-aunt worst of all, and is presumably why she hanged herself in the prison camp in 1945.

I found my great-grandmother's diary in my grandparents' loft. I had only Liva when I wrote the book. We all went to Berlin and found the family of the German soldier. Hans-Werner Meyer had died on the Eastern Front in 1942. His two sisters and a brother cried when I told them the story. They stroked my cheek and served us coffee in porcelain cups with blue flowers. My family was furious. They wanted me to forget the story, but I couldn't let go, and soon it was in all the papers. Mom didn't talk to me for six months.

I couldn't write any more after that experience.

Last year, I had planned to write a modern version of Strindberg's *Miss Julie*. When I first got the idea, I thought it was genius, but I'm less and less enthusiastic about it now. I can't even imagine a modern version of *Miss Julie*, probably because it's a stupid concept.

After the au pair started, I couldn't help thinking that I was right about saying that having help in the house wasn't really my thing. Well, partially right, at least, but

I'm never going to admit that. Now the house belongs to her. It's Ludmila who washes, who stacks the dishwasher, who makes the food. I should be working, but I've got nowhere to go. Whatever the case, it's perhaps high time I addressed the orgasm problem. These days I certainly have enough time to invest in it 100 percent.

I have no intention of letting it wait any longer. I want to grab the bull by the horns. I am going to dedicate this week to having an orgasm. How hard can it be?

I bought myself a vibrator with an orgasm guarantee. I tried to be honest when I was purchasing it. I stood outside Condomania on Main Street and waited until the shop was more or less empty.

I'd practiced beforehand what I was going to say in case I ran into anyone I knew. I could, for example, say that a friend of mine was having a bachelorette party, and that I was buying it for a laugh. But then again, they might think it was more embarrassing that I was buying it for fun rather than for what it is meant to do. The last time I went to a bachelorette party, it was clear that they all had vibrators and that it was quite normal to talk about it. They discussed the different kinds and sizes as if it was the most natural thing in the world. At the same party, a friend told us that she had gone home with a man, and when she woke up in his bed the next day, they had got up and walked down high street hand in hand. A gasp of disbelief spread throughout the group. Imagine holding hands with someone after a one-night stand! Feelings were problematic, but vibrators were totally normal.

THE GIRL BEHIND the Condomania counter was young, frighteningly so, but I decided to take the plunge anyway. I told myself that she probably dealt with people like me every day.

"Can I help you?" she said, in broad north Norwegian dialect.

She had a wide smiling mouth with artificially large lips.

"Yes. I've never had an orgasm. And I want to have one now."

There was silence for a few moments.

"Wow," was the girl's response.

"Quite," I said.

"Well, it's about time then," she said, regaining some of her salesmanship. "What you need is Mr. Rabbit. It's one of our bestsellers."

I looked skeptically at the pink toy she held out in front of me. The assistant appeared not to notice. She carried on, unperturbed, without drawing breath.

A rabbit, I thought. A rabbit that is going to be let loose between my thighs. I had a rabbit when I was little. It ate my dad's record collection, including all the Stones albums he was so proud of. It seemed a bit strange to let a nibbler loose in your most intimate region.

"It's made with a soft rubber material and has an attractive design, with cool metal balls. The balls rotate to stimulate the blood circulation in your vagina, which makes you more sensitive. There are six rotating speeds. The long rabbit ears that stimulate your clitoris have seven different speeds, or pulsating patterns, as they're called. You'll come before you're even turned on. Seriously!"

Presumably I still looked skeptical.

"Just touch it," she said, thrusting it over the counter.

I touched it. It felt alien.

"Oh, and we have an orgasm guarantee," the girl added.

"And how does that work?" I asked.

"When you a buy a vibrator from us, you get a thirty-day orgasm guarantee, which gives you adequate time to get to know the vibrator and test it out in peace and quiet. Let's face it, not all days are optimal for achieving orgasm. You need to allow yourself the time to try the product on a day when you're feeling a bit horny already. And you can redeem the orgasm guarantee in any of our shops if you've done all that and still don't feel that the particular model has met your needs," she told me, taking a deep breath.

I BOUGHT MR. RABBIT because I felt obliged. It would be stupid not to test it out, given the guarantee. But once we got home, I abandoned it. The time never seemed to be right to give it a try. The day when I was supposed to already be "a little bit horny" never came. There was always something with the children, or A, or both.

That was twenty-two days ago, and I now have only one week and one day before the guarantee expires.

One week should be enough. I've got time for that kind of thing now that we have an au pair. There was too much to do before, but now that Ludmila's here, I'm redundant in my own home. So, I'm going to masturbate while A is at work and the children are at school and preschool. Full-time. And I have no intention of stopping until I come. If people I meet ask me what I'm up to, that's exactly what I'm going to say.

"I'm masturbating full-time."

Of course I'm not actually going to say that, but it would be funny if I did.

On my bedside table, I have some cheese and flatbread, two bottles of water, four Paracetamol, a box of purple Läkerol liquorice, chewing gum, baby oil (unscented), lots of copies of *Dagbladet*, and a telephone. On the floor is a bucket to pee into. Nothing should disturb the mood. I don't want to ruin the build up to a possible orgasm because I need to go to the kitchen or the bathroom.

Dagbladet is the Norwegian newspaper that writes most about sex, not that I've carried out any extensive or systematic research. *VG* isn't too bad either, but *Dagbladet* writes a lot about female orgasms: how you can train your way to one, eat your way to one, or breathe your way to one. The idea is that I can read *Dagbladet* if I get a bit stuck.

DAY 1

THE DOOR IS locked. I'm lying on the bed with my eyes closed. I let the vibrator slide in between my legs and I try to enter into the spirit of my project.

"You are a sexually well-functioning woman," I tell myself in a hushed voice, as I frantically rub my clitoris.

The humming soon becomes a problem. It makes me think of my father — or my grandfather. The sound is exactly like their lawnmowers. I can almost smell the newly cut grass in the room, and taste the salt from my tears. I always cried when the cuckoo flowers got cut, which was usually when they were at their best and the ground was purple. I never understood why my father and grandfather had to do it right then. They wore big rain boots that were brown and seemed bigger than both of them. The last time I visited my grandparents, before Granddad died, his boots were standing in the hallway. He couldn't use them anymore. He hadn't been out of bed in a year. He was a thin old man, and the enormous boots that he used to wear seemed smaller, too.

Sometimes I long to age, so that I'm old enough to forget everything. I hope that I won't suffer; I hope that I won't miss anything, or anyone, because my memory has lapsed: that I won't miss the children I've borne, the houses I've lived in, or the men I've loved. I want to end up like a blank unwritten page, just as shameless as when I came into the world and heard my mother's screams. Surely I must have been without shame at that point? Maybe it's my shame that gets in the way of me coming?

I hope that the people who look after me do it with some warmth and are as unbusinesslike as possible. I hope that I'll be allowed to keep chocolate in a drawer in my bedside table, and that I won't feel ashamed when I have to be changed. I hope that I end up so deep in oblivion that no shame remains. When you have no shame, anything is possible.

My grandma got dementia. She forgot almost everything, just not her shame. It was as much a part of her as the psalms she had learned by heart as a child. I could see the shame deep down in her watery eyes. People said she was *away with the fairies*. "Poor thing, she's away," they said.

But my grandma was there. She sat in an armchair over by the window — the armchair from her house. The house with the big lawn that was always cut right when the cuckoo flowers were in full bloom. And while she sat there in the nursing home, in a chair that was no doubt vaguely familiar, no one cut the grass, and the cuckoo flowers covered the lawn in a thin veil. The uncut lawn was a sign of decline, Mom said, but the flowers were so beautiful. When the house was put up for sale, Dad cut the lawn and Mom washed away all signs of my grandparents. They gave us children the money they got for the house, so that we could buy ourselves new houses and apartments. I also got my grandfather's old teak desk, which is where I sit and write, or rather, where I sat when I *wrote*. I've written several books at that desk.

It's possible I'll live to a ripe old age — we do in our family. But I would rather die suddenly and unexpectedly, without shame.

DEATH! THAT'S WHAT the sound makes me think of. Is it surprising that it doesn't do it for me? Is it surprising then that I don't come? Despite Mr. Rabbit's orgasm guarantee, I've been lying here for over two hours thinking about death and cuckoo flowers, without anything happening. Nothing has happened! I think about my father, about my grandfather, about rain boots, about the desk, and get nowhere.

I try to think about the smell of asphalt instead. The

smell of freshly laid asphalt has always turned me on. Now why is that? I close my eyes.

It's between Christmas and New Year's. I'm thirteen. It's been a mild winter, and in those days, mild winters were a rare thing. I got a new, white, ribbed sweater for Christmas. And underneath it, my breasts are growing. It happens overnight, as if someone is inside my body working hard, moving fat and vulnerable material from one place to another. One day nothing, the next day something: two tender and fragile mounds filled with future freedom and autonomy.

The roads in our neighbourhood were being resurfaced, which was odd considering the time of year. An orange steamroller was parked in front of lit-up hedges. Men in orange coveralls, with spades in their hands, passed men in dark suits on their way to Christmas parties. I remember thinking how strange it is that anyone has to work over Christmas. There's no snow — it almost feels like spring — and we can't go skiing or sledding, so we're just there, hanging out on the street, watching the men pave the road.

"Out of the way, kids," one of the workmen says.

There are three older men and one slightly younger guy. I think it's an insult to be called a kid. I want to pull up my sweater and shout, "I'm not a kid!"

I go home and put on some makeup. I borrow Mom's blue eyeshadow and red lipstick. I put on a baseball cap and pull my ponytail out through the back. The outline of my budding breasts is visible through my new sweater, and my 501 jeans are full of holes. It's almost dark. I promise Mom I'll get the mail. The road is soft and new—oil and future, everything I will benefit from. A smell that tickles your nose. Only one of the workmen is still there. He's loading the equipment onto a truck. I want him to see me, to see that I'm not a kid. I dive deep into the mailbox with my hands to pull out the Christmas cards and Mom's Red Cross donation notice, and then I slam down the lid. The workman turns around and notices that there's someone there—and that someone is not a child.

He's not prepared for what comes next, or how easy it is, and how much I want it. I've read in books and magazines about how much it hurts the first time, but the pain is insignificant. It's all in your head, anyway. I'll have to decide for myself how I want to remember this moment. I'll decide if it doesn't hurt—or that the pain is insignificant. I straddle him in the driver's seat, without looking him in the eye. I'm cold, and burrow my nose into his orange coveralls. Then I watch a man come for the first time. He shrinks under me, swallows the noises that are on their way out. Somebody could walk by at any moment.

I think this is something I will do again, but then it won't be for the first time. It will never be the first time ever again.

"How old are you?" he asks.

He's back to normal now.

And I don't lie.

"Jesus Christ," he says, and pushes me away.

My sweater is ruined. It's got black oil smears on it that match the oil marks on my new breasts.

"What have you done to your sweater?" Mom shouts at me when I get home. I can't tell her it was my breasts that did it. Mom really should have asked where my flat bird chest had gone, where her child had gone.

And that is where the problems start. I've got so much to hide. It's impossible for me to be friends with my mom. Even though I really want to.

I had a childhood before the workman, but I stopped being interested in it a long time ago. I do what I can to forget it, not because it was painful or difficult in any way, but because I want to be an adult now. I've wanted to be an adult for as long as I can remember.

The old road through the neighbourhood had potholes that filled up when it rained. The old road made things stop. The asphalt made everything so much more efficient and so much more accessible—so possible. I sometimes forget what happened the day that the road was resurfaced, but I remember the smell of asphalt. It drops like a plumb line through my body whenever it reaches my nostrils.

I ONCE BOUGHT some cheap batteries from China. The children need batteries the way the rest of us need pants, which is why I bought those Chinese-made ones. They were ridiculously cheap for a ridiculous number of batteries, but then they only lasted for a few minutes each. I'm not joking. But today, I'm using proper batteries. I wouldn't want to take the risk. They just keep going and going. I've cleared my diary and set aside just over six hours to come today. That should be enough, unless there's something seriously wrong with me. But first things first.

The main problem is that I'm not entirely on my own. I'm alone in the room, and the door is locked, but Ludmila is wandering around up in the kitchen. What's to stop her climbing over the garden wall and breaking into the bedroom? It wouldn't be the first time. Once, when Ludmila had been with us no more than a week, I was woken by a noise outside the door, which opened onto the garden. We usually left it ajar at night. I'd often thought that anyone could just waltz in here, especially when we first moved in. Alva was a baby at the time, and there was a story in the *Aftenposten* about a woman in Oslo who was breastfeeding when burglars broke in and threatened her with a gun. I recalled that story every time I was feeding Alva. For a while, we slept with the door closed, but it got very stuffy, and A wasn't having it.

THE CLOCK RADIO on the bedside table says 2:05 a.m. when I hear the noise. I'm usually not frightened when A is there; it's as if his regular breathing could protect me and the children from everything. He sleeps so heavily that he wouldn't be good for anything before it was too late, but his being beside me makes me feel safer.

The noises from outside are fumbling, careful. Not at all threatening, really. Could it be an animal? A rat?

I'm not particularly fond of rats, but I would rather have it be a rat than a strange man outside the window. I give A a gentle nudge.

"A, wake up, there's something outside."

A rolls away to face the wall. I hear noises again and this time I have no doubt: something is pushing against the door. It's the kind of door that stops when you push the handle down, but it wouldn't be hard to force it open.

I shake A a little harder now, and he finally sits up in bed and looks at me indignantly. I watch the door being forced open and see a black foot slip into the room. I dive behind A's sleepy back before letting out a scream. I do think that it is perhaps not tactically wise to scream, but I do it all the same, and for some reason or another, I scream A's name.

The door gives way and a black figure tumbles into the room and hits the floor like a sack, right by the bed.

"A thousand sorry, a thousand sorry," the figure sprawled on the floor keeps saying.

It takes a few seconds before I see that it is Ludmila lying there. A says nothing. He turns on the light and squints at Ludmila, who mechanically repeats the same words.

"A thousand sorry, a thousand sorry."

"*What the hell?*" is the first thing A says.

"Are you crazy?" I scream.

"A thousand sorry," Ludmila says, as she gets up from the floor.

Her Ukrainian accent is enraging.

"Could you please say something other than that?!"

"Something other?" Ludmila looks at us.

I should probably feel sorry for her, but I'm not at the stage where I am concerned about her feelings yet. My heart is still hammering. How can I get back to sleep after this kind of incident?

"Explain yourself," I demand.

"I forgot my keys."

"It happens to the best of us," I say archly, "but you could have rung the bell."

"I not want to disturb."

"And this isn't disturbing us?"

"A thousand sorry," Ludmila says quickly.

"Will you stop saying that?!" I scream.

"I thought door to living room."

"Everyone makes mistakes," A says, with unexpected warmth in his voice.

A's warmth enrages me even more. I send him a look to suggest that I'm not finished with him yet, before asking Ludmila to go upstairs to bed.

"A thousand sorry," she says again and then tiptoes like an elephant up the stairs.

Martin sleeps like a log through the whole thing.

"Weren't you a bit hard on her?" A asks, as he turns out the light and rolls onto his side.

"Hard on her?"

I turn the light back on.

"What about the fact that I won't be able to sleep well ever again after this? I'll always be waiting for some madman to break down my bedroom door."

"She made a mistake, Julie, and she apologized."

"Lord only knows, she most certainly did! We might have been doing something private. We might have been having sex!"

"Right," A says, and turns off the light again.

I lie there staring at the billowing curtains. By the time Martin wakes up, I haven't slept a wink.

It's quite possible that Ludmila will storm through the door at any moment. How can I relax my body knowing that could happen? Of course I've locked the door, but the uncertainty has taken root; someone might come in, someone might see me. It's uncomfortable. Thinking about Ludmila doesn't really turn me on either. She's made my home feel unsafe and a place where it's impossible to relax. Is it surprising that I can't come?

And what's to stop A from doing the same? Maybe he's standing outside the door to the garden, trying to work out what's going on inside.

She's vacuuming at the moment. I should be pleased about that, but the noise from the vacuum cleaner is just as inhibiting as the noise from the vibrator. To be fair, it doesn't make me think about death, but I definitely associate it with my mother, and it's not easy to say which is worse right now.

I READ IN *Dagbladet* that as many as one in three women have never had an orgasm; the article is written by a journalist named Atle Jansen, and he's quoting Betty Dodson, a sexologist from the U.S. I eat some flatbread and cheese and drink some water. One in three women have not had an orgasm, but most women can *learn* how to reach orgasm, Atle Jansen writes. So there's hope for me. This is apparently true of both vaginal orgasm, which only about 10 percent of women achieve, and clitoral orgasm.

I read that the clitoris is — surprisingly — around thirteen centimetres long, but that most of it is not visible. There are roughly 8,000 nerve endings in the glans, or head, which is the visible part of the clitoris. That's about twice as many as in the head of the penis. There are two clitoral shafts that run along the vagina, which are stimulated when the penis penetrates. Atle Jansen writes that you have to discover whether you prefer to be touched on the left or right side of your clitoris, and that you have to observe what happens when you stimulate the clitoris with your finger. You should also focus on something else, preferably something sexy.

After I pee in the bucket beside the bed, I dig out my compact mirror and study my clitoris in detail. I can't get over the fact that it's thirteen centimetres long, and that it's more or less an iceberg, with the greater part hidden under the surface.

I wipe myself and carry on reading about how I should touch my breasts and tense my muscles and make noises. Some people prefer lying on their stomachs, whereas others prefer to lie on their backs. Atle Jansen reminds me to be mindful of my G spot. It's located just a few centimetres into the vagina, towards the stomach. He says you will notice the effect if your partner touches it on the downstroke at the same time that you, or your partner, press down hard on the pelvic bone.

My first thought is that I'm not abnormal. I'm one in three, one of many—perfectly normal. I can probably learn to reach orgasm. I just need to practice. So clearly I mustn't allow myself to be distracted, because it is not helpful to think of mothers and fathers and lawnmowers. And I must not think about Ludmila. On one level, that's not so strange. She's usually just one floor above me, but she's robbed me of my private life, and I'm not sure that I get enough in return. Isn't a messy house better than an occupied house?

When we knew that she was coming, I decided to get a cleaner in just once. If the house was in complete chaos when Ludmila arrived, she might think that that was how we lived. I explained this to A when I asked him to look for an agency.

"But that *is* how we live," he said.

"The point is that we have to give her a standard to start with. If the house is immaculate when she arrives, she'll think it's always like that."

A shook his head, but he arranged to have to the house cleaned.

The next day, two thin girls with Eastern European accents came to the door, carrying cleaning equipment and detergent. I didn't need to do anything other than let them in. I didn't want to look them in the eyes. I felt my cheeks burning. I was ashamed.

Everyone I knew had cleaners, so why was I the only one who felt ashamed?

Martin was dressed and ready in the stroller. I closed the door behind me and went out.

Everything was different when I got back four hours later. The house was unrecognizable. The clothes in the bathroom had been neatly folded, even if they were dirty. The surfaces and shower walls were gleaming. I wondered how they'd managed it. Perhaps A was right when he said that I couldn't clean. The shower walls had been grey for a long time now, verging on green because of the limescale. I had thought it was impossible to do anything about it.

A told me the visit from the cleaning ladies had cost 2,500 kroner, but it was worth it, I thought. Ludmila would come to a clean house where everything was in the right place. And that was the most important thing.

ON THE SATURDAY that Ludmila was due to arrive, I checked her room for the last time. Everything was in the right place. I had chosen to paint the room white and to use purple fabrics. The cushions had been chosen with great care, in lighter and darker shades of purple. The bedside table was from Room, and the small flat screen TV was brand new. The curtains were also purple. I had found the fabric at IKEA, and a neighbour had sewn the curtains for me. The double mattress was brand new as well. The room was, quite simply, lovely.

I would have been quite happy to move in there myself, but I couldn't. It was Ludmila's room, and I wanted her to have a room where she would be happy.

The wait was unbearable, but A was totally relaxed, of course. It was the afternoon.

"You should make pizza," he said. "She's bound to like that."

You certainly like pizza, I thought, grudgingly, but I made the dough and left it to rise. I actually enjoy making pizza on Saturday. It makes me feel like we're a perfectly normal, harmonious family that eats pizza together on a Saturday night.

When the doorbell finally rang, the pizza had been ready for a while, and A was circling around it like a starving wolf.

"Don't eat it!"

"Relax, you'd think we were expecting the king."

"It's important that she feels welcome, and that she understands it's an important day for us."

I felt my anticipation growing.

When the door swung open, I stood there with my jaw dropped.

In her photograph, she looked pious, like an innocent from the country. I had read that Ludmila was also the name of a Czech saint. On first impression, she was anything but saintly. Her long, brown hair from the photograph was now bleached, and feathered in a somewhat random fashion. She presumably didn't even pack the buttoned-up blouse that she wore in the photo because she was wearing a tight black top that left nothing to the imagination and revealed a pierced belly button. I felt a pang of disgust. Her previous host family had said nothing about her appearance.

Alva ran to meet her, whereas Liva held back.

"Come and say hello to Ludmila. She's going to live with us."

I could hear the strain in my voice, but Alva didn't seem to notice and was on her best behaviour. It warmed my heart to see it. Alva was so incredibly beautiful with her fair curls, but Ludmila wasn't affected in the slightest. She barely glanced at my beaming little fairy.

"This is Alva," I said, my voice a touch sharp, as though to remind Ludmila why she was here.

A sauntered out of the kitchen, smiling. His hello was relaxed and open. If he was disappointed by Ludmila's appearance, he certainly didn't show it. I thought I should behave in the same way, because it wasn't Ludmila's appearance that mattered, but how could you dress like that and be a reliable person? I wasn't convinced it was possible.

I gave Liva a stern look, and she came forward to say hello, looking very skeptical. I couldn't blame her.

"Do you have any luggage?"

"Yes," Ludmila replied. She turned around, opened the front door and talked fast and frantically into the dark. And then Michael, one of the Polish workers who had built her sleeping platform, came in wearing horribly muddy shoes and carrying two medium-size suitcases. I couldn't really explain to him that we'd just spent 2,500 kroner to wash the floors.

Michael was making me uneasy. He and Ludmila

exchanged several remarks in Russian; they laughed and looked at me. The whole welcome had been ruined. I felt like an outsider — excluded — even though it was *my* home and *my* welcome.

I had been waiting for this moment for two months. I had envisioned that I would show care, forbearance, and love, but was doing nothing of the sort now. Michael laughed loudly and winked with one of his amber eyes, and I felt confused and slightly paranoid.

Was Michael laughing at me?

I moved closer to A and picked up Martin, who had crawled over. I held him in front of me like a shield and said a little too loudly: "And this is Martin."

Ludmila barely glanced at Martin either. She looked at Michael who kissed her once on each cheek before saying something in Russian and disappearing. I felt a burst of irritation and wanted to shout that they had to speak Norwegian when they were in my house. But instead I just repeated, "This is Martin."

"Hello," Ludmila said, pinching his cheek so his lower lip drooped. He rubbed his face against my shoulder.

I swallowed.

"Can I show you your room?"

"Yes," Ludmila replied. Her voice was deep and husky.

I tried to keep a brave face. The room was perfect, after all. It was the most thought-out room in the whole house. I looked at Ludmila expectantly when I somewhat dramatically threw open the door. It took a while before she said anything.

"Is bed up there?" she asked eventually.

I nodded.

Ludmila sighed.

"We hope you like the room."

"It's okay," Ludmila said.

"You've got a TV up there as well."

"Oh, I don't watch so much TV," she remarked, and put her suitcases down in the corner with a shrug.

There was no gratitude, no joy at meeting the children or seeing the lovely room. What had I done? What was I going to do with a person who wasn't able to show any enthusiasm or love?

A looked as though he guessed what I was thinking.

"Perhaps she imagined she would get something else after seven years at university."

"Seven years of *pedagogy*. Don't you study pedagogy because you want to work with children?"

A just smiled and shrugged. Even though he made no protest, I got the feeling he thought he was right.

DAY 2

LUDMILA AND MARTIN have gone out. I run up to the kitchen and make myself some food. Jam and mackerel in tomato sauce are the only things in the fridge. I must ask Ludmila to pull up her socks on the shopping front. I clean a carrot and take half a cucumber that I can use to experiment with. I also take the opportunity to make some coffee, which I pour into a thermos. I take the thermos, the carrot, the cucumber, and some sandwiches back down into the bedroom with me. I'm ready. Everything is in place. I lie down and slide the cucumber in between my legs.

The cucumber smells of summer. Mom used to make cucumber salad with trout during the warm months when Dad went fishing every week, and was out all night and came home at dawn, with starry eyes and a pair of trout hanging from his belt. Mom didn't approve of these fishing trips. She always said that Dad didn't go on fishing trips to fish, but to be with his friends and stay up all night. I never knew what she really meant when she said, "stay up all night," but when dinner was served on Sunday, she was always happy. She was always praised for the way she prepared the trout, and the pepper sauce she served with it, not to mention her cucumber salad. Dad's eyes shone and his cheeks were red. He tickled her waist and made her giggle like a schoolgirl.

I give up on the cucumber. What a stupid idea! After all, I've got a better toy, one with an orgasm guarantee. And what's more, these cucumbers from abroad might be sprayed with all kinds of insecticides that are not good for the body.

I hear Ludmila and Martin come in upstairs. They must have forgotten something. I can't get used to having someone in the house who just comes and goes as she pleases. Right now it's hard to understand why I wanted an au pair so much. I searched for her with much the same pleasure and enthusiasm as I'd had when I looked for a dog as a child.

I was ten when I suddenly decided that I wanted a dog, more like I *had* to have a dog. I spent days and weeks in the library looking for the right breed. I thought beagles were the sweetest. In one book, I found a photograph of two beagle puppies in a basket. They were so beautiful. I wanted nothing in the world more than a beagle puppy. The problem was that Mom and Dad said no. Dad was particularly unreasonable. It was a flat no. I was too young to look after a dog, he said, and he would end up taking the dog out in all kinds of weather when I got bored of it.

I snorted at all his objections. He thought that I wouldn't walk the dog. A beagle? I would love that dog; I would do anything for it. I couldn't think of anything other than the dog. I lay awake at night and fantasized about my life with a beagle; it was impossible to sleep. I got bags under my eyes and fell asleep at my desk at school.

Mom was close to breaking. I begged and pleaded. I would clean the house every Friday, and stack the dishes every day. I would do anything—anything—I was asked. Mom almost started to believe me. She really wanted to say yes, I could tell, but Dad was in the way. He talked about something called "empirical knowledge."

"Empirical knowledge would indicate that it will never happen," he said.

Help came from an unexpected source. One Saturday, Granddad appeared in the living room with a brown basket, not so unlike the one in the picture in the book. When Granddad made up his mind about something, not even Dad stood in his way. It was Granddad who decided, since he was above Dad in the pecking order. When my parents moved here, he gave them the house they lived in, the car Dad drove to work in, and even the job he drove to. Granddad was someone who knew which strings to pull. There was nothing Dad could say, and I knew that, and smiled triumphantly at him before burrowing my nose in the soft dog fur. It was a bitch. I named her Maika after the girl in the children's TV series *She Came Out Of The Blue Sky*.

The first few weeks were like something out of a fairy tale. I took Maika for walks. It was the end of September and the trees slowly turned to flaming golden red. The autumn rain had not set in. Everyone in my class wanted to come with us. At school, Linda sat beside me. Linda with the long, fair braids wanted to sit beside me and come home with me after school. I realized it was because of the dog. Everyone wanted to write in my yearbook. Mom had found me a book with a picture of three beagle puppies on the front. Linda wrote first, then Monica, then Marianne.

After a few weeks, all this attention waned. Other things took over. The new girl, who had just moved from Oslo, had an angora rabbit in a cage in her room. Linda didn't come home with me anymore. It started to rain. And it didn't stop. It wasn't the same, going for walks in the rain. November was cold and wet. The trees looked naked and threatening. I stopped going for walks. In the mornings, I only took Maika behind the house for a pee. The dog wasn't cute any more. She had grown so quickly and was almost full grown.

Dad scrutinized me at mealtimes; he already had that "I told you so" look. The situation started to become unbearable.

On one of my short walks in the neighbourhood, I discovered an open manhole cover. Later that evening I took Maika with me and forced the struggling dog down into the black hole. There must have been water at the bottom, because I heard a splash. She didn't make a sound. She didn't bark and whine the way I thought she would. There was just a plop. I almost managed to get the cover back on and then ran like mad. It was pitch black and I tripped and hit my knee on the asphalt. It hurt and I got a hole in the new Levi's that I'd finally been allowed to buy. Everyone helped me look; Linda even skipped a gymnastics display in the gym hall to assist. For a moment, I regretted what I'd done, but mostly, I felt enormous relief. I was free.

Mom fell for it, of course, and was full of sympathy and love. She could not even begin to imagine what I'd done. Dad was the problem. He stared at me as though he knew. Obviously, he helped to look like everyone else he searched and shouted: "Maika! Here girl, heel, heel…Maika!" But he said it like he didn't believe it. His calls were half-hearted, as though he knew that I had already got rid of the dog in the most horrible way. Apart from that, there were no problems. The girls in the class felt sorry for me because I'd lost my dog. I almost felt sorry for myself as well, but the feeling of freedom was intoxicating, at least as intoxicating as the first time I'd held Maika in my arms.

WHEN IT CAME to finding the au pair, I studied websites on the Internet just as vigorously as I had once trawled the library in search of dog books. (Little did I know that I would have the same feeling of intoxication on the day I got rid of the au pair as when I'd got rid of the dog.) And little did I know that I would go to bed that night and dream about Maika, my falling dog. I've never told anyone about it, not even A. I assumed that people would be disgusted. I don't think I know anyone else who could do such a thing. But you never know. Whatever the case, I haven't told a soul. I was just a child, after all.

Everyone I knew who'd ever had an au pair highly recommended Filipino girls, but I didn't want some servile shadow who did what she was told and was always happy. I wanted someone who spoke Norwegian, and who could communicate with the children. Maybe someone from Eastern Europe.

I composed an advert for the website *Au Pair World*, where I tried to portray the family as honestly as possible. Could I say, "We are a harmonious family"? The only thing we really argued about was housework and looking after the children. We would be a harmonious family as soon as those issues were a thing of the past. I wrote that we were a harmonious family. It was true. It would certainly be true the moment someone moved in to look after the children and do the housework.

We have a small garden outside the house. Where I come from, no one would call it a garden. Mom would laugh to hear me refer to it as a garden, but fifty square metres of grass in the centre of Oslo surely counted as a garden. I wrote "garden." Own entrance? There was a door from the deck into my office. If you wanted to use it, you would have to move the trash cans. And the lock on the door was broken, but it was still a door: an entrance and an exit. I wrote: "room with separate entrance." The neighbour also had an au pair. It seemed to work fantastically. She was good with the children and worked like trooper in the house. And still she seemed to be part of the family. That's what I wanted as well. I wrote that we were looking for someone who could become part of our family.

"Harmonious family of five looking for a new family member. We can offer flexible working hours and a room with a separate entrance. We live in the centre of Oslo and have a garden. There are several other au pairs in the neighbourhood." (Translation: the neighbour's au pair is on her way to Bergen to study, but they're getting a new one.)

In the course of a week, we received over a hundred responses. Had I embellished the truth a little too much? One applicant was a cardiologist, another a linguist. Wouldn't it just be fantastic to have our own doctor in the house? Our own cardiologist? When I first read her application, I was full of enthusiasm. The cardiologist wrote that she had plenty of experience looking after children because she was an aunt. Her page was full of photographs of her taking care of and playing with a thin, slight, and pale child who looked like a Romanian orphan. The cardiologist herself was tall and quite attractive — not too attractive — but just right. I obviously didn't want anyone ugly in the house, but the au pair couldn't be too good-looking either. After all, A got so little sex that it might be a bit risky.

When I went to bed, I was convinced that I would write to the cardiologist and offer her the job, but when I sat down at the computer the following day, my thoughts turned to all the potential problems. Wouldn't it seem a bit ridiculous to ask a cardiologist to wash the floor? Could I talk to a cardiologist with any authority and say things like, "Please could you wash my underpants?" No, I wasn't so sure. My family, especially my mother, held doctors in the highest esteem. I therefore also had the utmost respect for doctors. A was of the view that doctors were also people and that poking around in various body orifices, wading through irritable patients with flu, and being late all the time were not particularly attractive job requirements. He didn't understand what it is about doctors. We had no doctors in the family. We had priests, professors of one sort of another, but no one in medicine. We needed a doctor.

But why would a cardiologist want to come to Norway? I asked myself. Certainly not to look after my children. The cardiologist must have another reason. No doubt she wanted to learn Norwegian and be a cardiologist here. She must not be interested in children at all, and definitely not mine, so how could I then leave them in her care?

I decided to wait until a pediatrician applied, but the days passed and no pediatrician appeared. The torrent of applications started to dwindle. I complained to A, who said there had to be *someone* who was suitable among the 132 applicants. I tried to explain to him that that wasn't necessarily the case. They were either over- or under-qualified.

I checked my account on *Au Pair World* every day. The time between applications got longer and longer, but they kept coming in. When I got Ludmila's application it was already October, and there was a thin layer of ice on the pavement when I reluctantly took Alva to preschool. The air was damp and chilly, and Martin's little hands, which stuck out of his winter snowsuit, were frozen. He refused to wear mittens and I'd given up trying. I was sick and tired of picking them up from the street.

It wasn't so easy to take him to the park anymore. His snowsuit and winter boots restricted him. There was too much to put on and take off. And every day I thought that I couldn't bear it any more. I needed to get him a spot in preschool. And on that October day, I read Ludmila's application and thought it was just what I'd been waiting for.

Ludmila was a trained teacher. She spoke Norwegian because she had already been with a family in Norway for a year. She had taught English to Ukrainian children. In her photograph she looked like a girl with no style, but she looked clean and proper. She had long, straight dark hair and bangs. Her white blouse was buttoned all the way up. The picture didn't show whether she was fat or thin, but I guessed she was perhaps a little chubby and was therefore unlikely to be a threat. She wasn't a doctor, but she was a teacher. At least it was something to do with children, I told myself. Teacher was good. And she had a friendly smile—an inclusive and warm smile, perhaps even a positive smile. Ludmila. The name made me think of a Russian prostitute, but Ludmila was clearly no prostitute. It was Ludmila I wanted. When I googled her name, I discovered that Ludmila was a Czech saint. Saint Ludmila.

I called her former family the same evening. As expected, they had only positive things to say about her. She was conscientious and nice. Good with the children. I counted my lucky stars.

It would be so unbelievably nice to leave the house-work to someone else, so that I could get my freedom back. I could no longer remember what it was like to just leave, close the door behind me and feel free. Ludmila could not start for another month, but that didn't matter.

UPSTAIRS, THE DOOR slams. Exit Ludmila and Martin. I'm alone again.

I put down the cucumber and grab the vibrator instead. It tickles and is most definitely pleasant. Is that how an orgasm starts? With a tickling sensation?

Again I am struck by the absurdity of the situation. Why have I not had an orgasm before?

Could it be because I experienced something as a child, something that is blocking my orgasms? Something that makes me shut down? Is that the problem?

I was seven the first time I heard the word *sex*. It seemed to be problematic. It was quite obviously something you didn't talk about. I was lying under the kitchen table at my grandparents' house. An old lady from the neighbourhood was visiting. She was often there. She had grey hair that was usually pulled into a tight bun, and a golden Labrador that I adored. She had lived alone since the death of her mother, whom she had cared for. She had loosened her grey hair on the day I was hiding under the table, and to my surprise, it reached down to her waist.

Her hands were shaking as she held one of Grandma's English teacups.

"He took his clothes off?"

Grandma's voice was agitated and aghast.

"Yes, everything. He only had his socks on. The rest of his clothes were lying in a heap. He ran off in just his socks."

"How awful," Grandma exclaimed.

It was October. I couldn't imagine why anyone would want to go running wearing only their socks.

"If it hadn't been for her, I don't know what might have happened," the guest sighed, as she nodded at her dog and gave her a ginger biscuit.

Grandma made ginger biscuits once a year and kept them in airtight tins at the back of the pantry. They were generally offered to unexpected guests. I had never seen anyone give one of the biscuits to a dog. Grandma would not have liked it, but she didn't even notice.

"What did he want?"

"He certainly didn't want money. My purse was lying on the table and he didn't touch it."

"Sex? Is that what he wanted?"

The woman must have nodded.

"Oh, that's just awful," Grandma said again.

I remember thinking that surely it was a good thing that he didn't want money and didn't touch the purse.

"I had been asleep. It was terrible shock."

"Of course, of course. But he didn't, um, get his way?"

"No. The dog scared him off."

"Thank goodness for the dog!"

Grandma leaned down to look at the dog under the table, because she deserved acknowledgement. I was petrified that I'd be discovered. By then, I had realized that this was something I was not supposed to hear.

Later in the day, I asked Mom what had happened. She just made a shush sound, trying to brush me off. It wasn't important, she said, and then explained that she had to get dinner in the oven. Not all mothers were like my mother.

"Rape," said Trude in my class.

"Attempted rape," Thomas corrected her.

Why should that frighten me? Surely it just made me more curious.

I think it might have had something to do with the flasher. When I was growing up there was a flasher where we lived. Our mothers were terrified of him. We children, on the other hand, thought he was funny. He always wore a tartan coat and could be found around the parks and community centres, rain or shine. He had a childlike face, but his body was so big and strong it looked almost disconnected from his head.

Sometimes he gave us sweets. I was one of the few who accepted. I've never been able to say no to sweets. Lots of the girls in my class thought it was too dangerous to say yes. He would want something back, they said. I wasn't so sure.

I officially met him one Tuesday evening after swimming. I had my wet swimsuit and towel in a sports bag over my shoulder, and my matted hair in a ponytail. I had to go through an underpass on my way from the swimming pool to my house. It wasn't nice walking there at night. It smelled of piss and all the sounds seemed closer and sharper.

"Touch it!"

He came from nowhere and stood in the middle of the tunnel, blocking out the street lights at the other end.

"Touch it," he repeated.

His voice was raspy and tense, impatient.

He had opened his tartan coat and he was naked underneath. When he moved slightly to the left, he let the beam from the street lights into the underpass so I could see that his enormous gut almost covered his tiny, flaccid willy.

I closed my eyes and walked straight past him, my heart exploding in my chest and ears, echoing in the underpass.

I don't know what I had expected — perhaps that he would hold me back against my will, that he would force me to touch it — but he did nothing. All I could hear behind me was his heavy breathing. Then I was free.

I carried on walking without turning around. The first thought that popped into my head in the wake of my ebbing fear was *poor man; poor, pathetic man.* I was twelve years old. I knew nothing about how things worked, but I had recognized wretchedness and the fact that a man could, and in many cases would, do whatever was needed to have girls touch and look, and then lose control.

My first boyfriend was the most popular boy in the school. Everyone thought he was going to be a professional football player. He could have gone out with whomever he wanted, but for reasons I never understood, he chose me. He was clearly not a flasher, but he said the same thing.

"Touch it," he said.

I didn't want to touch it. I didn't like to see him beg like a dog. I'd already experienced a thing or two. I'd given myself to a complete stranger who was laying asphalt on the street where I lived, and I'd done it of my own free will. I did it because he didn't beg.

Of course I could touch my boyfriend. I just didn't want him to beg.

Even back then, I was already very practical. We were standing in the bathroom at his house. He had been to practice and was about to shower.

"Come into the bathroom with me," he said.

I did and he took his clothes off. He begged me to touch him and I refused. I said his mom would have me charged.

"Forget Mom," he said.

But I couldn't, and I didn't want to touch him.

"Just a bit," he pleaded.

"No," I said.

He had a shower and was himself again. We said nothing more about it, but I mused that it had been much easier to walk past the flasher in the underpass. It had been the right thing to do. You shouldn't touch a flasher's willy. But the incident in the bathroom made me feel inferior. Should I have touched it? After all, we were going out.

A week later he dumped me. I was really upset and concluded that I should have touched it. I asked myself what he would have said if he knew about the asphalt man. I had problems sleeping at night. It was often four in the morning before I stopped playing solitaire and turned off the light. I walked around in a daze. Everyone thought I was suffering from a broken heart, but I wasn't so sure.

Then, a month after the breakup, the flasher appeared again. The situation was identical to the previous time. I was on my way home from swimming with my wet ponytail slapping against my back. He stood there with his coat open in the dark underpass.

"Touch it," he said.

I didn't find the situation frightening this time. I walked up to him very calmly and put my hand on his little prick. It felt like it shrank even more when I touched it. It was no more than a couple seconds before he wrapped his coat around himself and ran off. I think I heard him crying.

After that, I slept like a rock.

I THINK ABOUT the girl at Condomania. The one who sold me Mr. Rabbit.

She said exactly the same as the flasher and my first boyfriend.

"Just touch it."

I put Mr. Rabbit down. Rabbits do it quickly and efficiently. If you fuck like a rabbit, it's fast, but so far nothing has happened.

It's not going to happen, I think, but is that so awful? Why is it embarrassing that I can't do it? Why can't I just talk about it with my friends?

Is it that important to talk about things? The woman who sat at my grandma's table eating ginger biscuits, frightened and shaken by a man who had broken into her home, was not used to talking about sex. She had never lived with a man. I don't even think she'd ever had a boyfriend. She had lived her life alone, with her dog, but she had friends; she had my grandma to eat ginger biscuits with. Before she retired, she had written a book about weaving. I remember that she was a very good weaver. Grandma was proud to know her. Was her life worth nothing because she didn't have sex? Because she couldn't talk about sex?

When I was younger, I had conversations about orgasms with my friends, but over the years, these have tailed off. When Cecilie first met her architect husband, she used to say things like: "God, he's amazing! I came four times yesterday."

"Are you sure about that?" I might inquire.

"You know when you've had an orgasm!"

"'Yes, if you're not sure whether you've had an orgasm, then you've definitely not had one," I agreed.

I don't know whether I've had an orgasm, therefore I haven't had one.

And suddenly I realize that Mr. Rabbit's orgasm guarantee means nothing. How likely is it that I would go down to Condomania and say to the presumably sexually well-functioning nineteen-year-old behind the counter: "It didn't work. Give me my money back."

"What do you mean, it didn't work?" she might answer. "Was there something wrong with the beads?"

"I didn't come," I could answer, and then she would have to give me detailed advice and tips on how to use it properly or give me my 698 kroner back, and everyone behind me in the line would know that I'm a failure as a woman.

A HUNDRED YEARS ago, women were not supposed to have any sexual desire. Desire was scandalous. A woman who made choices on the basis of who she desired was isolated and punished—or she punished herself. For example, Anna Karenina threw herself in front of a train. Today it's a scandal *not* to have any desire—not so scandalous that people throw themselves in front of trains, but you never know. The shame has shifted. It might be moving slowly, but it's moving.

I NEED SOME fresh air. And I'm hungry. I want something to eat other than jam or mackerel in tomato sauce. I venture out to the supermarket, where I come across an amusing zucchini. It's organic and slightly bent. I assume that if I have a G spot, this zucchini will be able to find it for me. It is absolutely worth a shot. At least if this zucchini works, it will be more environmentally friendly than Mr. Rabbit, with all his metal beads and pulsing. I optimistically pop the vegetable into my basket.

BACK HOME IN bed, I have to say the zucchini is actually rather pleasant. The Condomania's orgasm guarantee can bow its head in shame because I soon discover that a 20-kroner vegetable from the supermarket gives much better results. A zucchini is silent, which means that you can concentrate in a completely different way.

There is no humming that reminds you of fathers and lawnmowers.

My juices are flowing. The baby oil was completely unnecessary. It does strike me that it probably feels so good because I didn't have any expectations. The vibrator, along with its guarantee, only put pressure on me and made me think that I would never be able to come if I couldn't succeed with Mr. Rabbit. "Freshness" was the only guarantee I got for the zucchini. I think that's why it's working.

I'm moaning instinctively. I think it's is helping me along and allowing me to let go. I'm surprised by how easy it can be: I'm going to come!

"Julie?" I hear a voice call out.

Typical! Just when I was doing so well.

Camilla, the neighbour, is upstairs in the hall. She apologizes, but it's not particularly polite of her to just walk into someone else's house.

"Sorry if I'm interrupting."

I assure her that she's not disturbing me at all.

"I wondered if you had any vegetables I could borrow? I've got a colleague coming over for lunch, and I've completely forgotten to buy any sides."

"I'm not sure what we have. I lose track a bit more now that we have the au pair. What do you need?"

"A cauliflower, a red pepper, or a zucchini?"

"I *do* have a zucchini," I say, somewhat hesitantly.

"Would you mind if I borrowed it? I'll buy you another one this evening. I just don't have time to go to the store right now."

"It is not a problem. Give me a minute."

I rinse the zucchini under the tap, dry it with paper towel, and take it out into the hallway.

"It's very bent."

"It's organic," I say, handing it over.

"Thanks a million," Camilla says, before dashing back to her kitchen.

I'm not sure I'll find another one that good in the shop, and curse my generosity.

LUDMILA AND MARTIN are back from their walk. Martin is crying and Ludmila is speaking to him in Russian. What is she saying? This was not part of the deal. Martin has to learn to speak Norwegian before he starts to learn a Slavic language, which was precisely the reason I chose Ludmila and not someone from the Philippines. But then again, Ludmila's Norwegian isn't particularly good either. What if Martin ends up with her pronunciation? It's not easy to say which would be worse for Martin — learning a Slavic language before Norwegian or learning to speak Norwegian with a Ukrainian accent — but it's definitely something I have to discuss with her when I get time. I try not to think about Martin's language development and instead to focus on the task at hand.

I *will* have an orgasm. It will happen this week.

"What have you been up to today?" A asks when he gets home.

"Nothing in particular," I reply.

But tomorrow I'll have a different answer to the same question. I will be able to say, "Today I had an orgasm."

DAY 3

THE DAY DOESN'T start well. I wake up and there's a smell of poo in the air. The clock radio on the bedside table shows 5:50 a.m. I can hear Alva breathing in the living room. A is sleeping — heavily. A always sleeps heavily. It's almost like he can press a button and fall instantaneously asleep. It's much harder for me. I have to somehow mix sleep carefully into every part of my body. It makes no difference whether I'm tired or not. I can be so tired that I can't sleep. If Martin so much as moves, I wake up. The children are in my blood.

I get out of bed like a robot. Alva is sitting on the sofa under her duvet, her eyes glazed over.

"Do you need a poo?"

She shakes her head. I pull back the duvet and discover that there's shit everywhere.

"Alva," I reprimand her. "We've talked about this. If you need the toilet, you have to tell us."

"It was an accident," she says, defiantly.

I lift her up, holding her far from my body. Something falls onto the floor. I step in it, but don't slip, and yell for A, who comes out drunk with sleep and slips in the mound.

We both laugh in the end, since there's nothing else that can be done. Then all three of us head into the shower. We all laugh. Miraculously, Martin continues sleeping like a log. We dry each other's bodies. A makes faces and we carry on laughing. We look like a family in an American film about the meaning of life, playing around, laughing, and being close to the ones we love.

Once we're dried and dressed again, we plunk Alva down in front of Disney Channel, which thankfully starts broadcasting at 6 a.m. Martin wakes up. I kiss him and put him down beside his sister, who puts her arm around him far too roughly. Liva isn't up yet, but she has to go to school in an hour and a half, and she needs a packed lunch.

A strokes my back. The sound of Mickey Mouse Clubhouse burbles in the background: "Come inside, it's fun inside..." I know what that hand wants. It's seemingly innocent, but I know its true intentions. If I say that I don't want to have sex, he'll get irritated. He'll explain that he was only stroking my back—that's all—and then will turn away in anger. The day will be ruined before it's even started. I don't want it to be that way, but that's how it turns out.

"You want sex now? After we've been rolling in shit?"

He turns his back and falls asleep. I could have used the opportunity as a kind of foreplay, but I have a very long day in bed ahead of me.

I get up because it's impossible to sleep. I pull the cover off the sofa in the living room and put everything in a black garbage bag. I'll have to get it to the dry cleaner as soon as possible.

I hear Ludmila turn on the kettle up in the kitchen. I wake Liva. I'm still in my bathrobe. Ludmila and I say a guarded good morning. A is not particularly happy after our early start, but he smiles to Ludmila and she smiles back.

Ludmila puts Martin in the stroller and goes for a walk so he falls asleep. A takes Alva to preschool; Liva goes to school. Ludmila comes back and starts the housework. I go to bed as soon as she comes in, and we say nothing to each other. On one level I understand that she wants to get rid of me, the way other au pairs get rid of their employers during the day, but I've got no plans to go anywhere. I'm not going out. I'm going to stay here because I'm going to come. And she'll just have to deal with it.

M Y FIRST REAL boyfriend looks like a child, but is in fact twice my age. He works in a big shipyard where they build oil platforms. He works with his hands.

My first real boyfriend drinks. I'm sixteen. I'm convinced he'll be able to stop; he just needs to choose otherwise. It's not as simple as I think.

He's constantly surrounded by girls and women because he's so good-looking. He's not to be trusted. He already has a child with another woman. A charming child that I make an effort with, initially for my boyfriend's sake, but later for the child's sake. I want him to see how good I am, what I can do for his child. I think that maybe it will make him love me more.

He loves me in his own way, in the only way he can love anyone, but he's not to be trusted. I'm too little, too young, to get into the bars and restaurants in town. When he goes there, he's cut off from me, unreachable.

Sometimes I stand outside waiting. Sometimes I get so anxious that I ask an acquaintance or random passerby to go in to the pool hall to get him for me. When he comes out, he usually says that I should go home. His eyes are evasive.

"Go home to your parents," he says, as though I'm an inconvenience, and have nothing to do with him.

I do as he says—go home to Mommy and Daddy. I bury my nose in the fur of a cat that I found on the street and cry, until Mom is beside herself and doesn't know what to do. I just want to die. A cat is different from a dog. A cat comes and goes. I feel as though I have two of them.

Other times he asks me to go back to his house and wait. He gives me the key ring with a leather football fob.

His house is small. The mother of his child used to live there with him. It's obvious a woman previously inhabited the house. The furniture is old and inherited, so presumably she's taken anything of any value with her. He's not interested in furniture; he doesn't blame her. Not for *that*. But he does blame her for the state she left him in. The black hole that he fills with increasing amounts of alcohol. She's taken the child with her and he can't love it on his own. Loving a child is work for two, he says.

It is my mission to save him, to pull him out of the

hole. I dress and decorate him, just as I will decorate numerous apartments later in life. He is my project. I don't care about anything else at this point. Only him.

I lie in the enormous king-size bed and wait for the pubs and bars to close. I read Sylvia Plath, Marguerite Duras, and Selma Lagerlöf. I try to find something that mirrors my experience. In a strange way, I'm growing, but no one can see, no one is concerned about the same things as me. It's a separate reality, a kind of happiness.

When he comes home, we have sex. He calls it *making love*. I'm not used to the phrase. It makes me giggle. It's not impossible that it's love I feel, but sex is still something technical, something I can be better at, something I want to master. I like it, but I don't orgasm.

Sometimes I threaten him, as I will later threaten my children. I'm sixteen years old. I know nothing of the children who will arrive with the future, but the threats don't work on him, and they won't work on my eventual children either.

"If you don't stop drinking, I'll leave you," I say. But he doesn't stop drinking, and I don't leave him. He realizes that after a while.

Like when I say to my children: "If you don't go to bed, there will be no candy on Saturday." But they still don't go to bed, and when Saturday rolls around they get candy all the same. They realize this after a while.

I want to change him, but nothing works. I haven't got any cards left to play, just sex. I reward and punish him as much as possible with my weapon. I'm fully aware of the power I have, denying him what he needs most at the exact moment he wants it.

The girls in my class are sixteen. I want to be like them, apparently without a worry in the world, but it's too late. I can already do too much and know too much. Nothing will ever be the same. It's too late; we will never be alike.

I TRY TO establish why.

Why does he drink?

He's good-looking, relatively intelligent. He wasn't bullied at school. He's good at football. His dad, on the other hand...

I come to the conclusion that it's genetic. His father is a drinker and gets into fights. His mother can't do anything about it, and he beats her, too. He's not like his father. My boyfriend is gentle as a lamb, but he drinks, just as his father does.

I already know that we're not going to end up together, that my real future lies somewhere else. I'm going to go the University of Oslo after secondary school is finished. In ten years' time, I'll be a completely different person. I know that, but sometimes I forget. When he's lying in my arms, shaking after a binge, I paint a rosy picture of the future for him. How he can start again when he's done with alcohol and go to college to learn new things. And he lets himself get carried away. Sometimes he cries. He lies in my arms and cries.

In ten years' time, I'll be different. In ten years' time, he'll be dead.

SINCE I WAS very little, I've had a recurring dream about going to the fair and winning a big teddy bear. In my early teens, it was my boyfriend who would win the bear for me, and we would walk hand in hand through the fairground, the bear under my arm. It was a ridiculous dream. As a sixteen-year-old I knew that, but I still held on to it.

Every year, a fair set up on the gravel pitch that was usually used for football, by the abandoned school. I like fairs, the change they represent, how the pitch is transformed into an explosion of colour and noise, how the smells of oil, candyfloss, and popcorn blend with lilac and spring. It's always colder than you think it's going to be; you always freeze, but still don't go home, and end up with cystitis.

The fair arrives like clockwork the first spring we're together. I think that it's finally going to happen—he's going to win a bear for me. He'll hit the bull's eye or throw a ball at tin cans. It doesn't really matter *how* he does it, only it can't be a raffle, because I can also be lucky. There's something masculine about winning. I want someone to fight and win something on my behalf because I should be weak and he should be strong.

After school, I run up to the fairground to wait for him. It's Friday, the first Friday in May. Spring is all around and I'm giddy and happy. It's not raining and everything is as it should be. He's supposed to finish work at four, and then he has to clock out and put his work boots in his locker. We agreed to meet here at five. He'll be freshly showered with his pay packet in his back pocket.

He doesn't come. Deep down, I knew that he wouldn't, or at least was scared that he wouldn't. Deep down, I know the whole teddy bear thing is stupid. The girls from my class go with their football boyfriends. They all look so happy. Right there and then, I yearn to be one of them, even though I know it's impossible.

I meet him later in the centre of town. He's drunk. He's completely forgotten all about the fair, forgotten our date, and forgotten me. He's drunk up most of his pay. There won't be any money left to go to the fair the next day. And in any case, it's too late. I don't want a teddy bear anymore.

MONEY IS ALWAYS a problem. He doesn't like working. He hates his job. During some football championship, he threatens to break his thumb with a hammer so he can stay home from work. He wants me to do it.

"You do it," he says, and puts his thumb on the block.

I tell him I could never do that.

"Then I'll do it myself," he asserts.

I don't doubt for a moment that he will.

"Okay, I'll do it."

I don't want to do it, but say yes to bide time, to stop him from doing it himself. He closes his eyes, catches his breath, and puts the hammer in my hand.

"Hit me hard. You're tough. That's why I love you."

He's never said that he loves me before. I feel happy and confused.

Before the hammer hits, I don't believe that I've got it in me.

That's how much I love him, I think.

His thumb is crushed, broken. I cry like a baby. He takes some slugs of moonshine before he goes to the emergency room. He gets sick leave and watches football and drinks for two weeks. That's what makes him happy. And I'm happy if he's happy.

SOMETIME LATER, HE stops working and somehow manages to claim disability. I don't know how he does it, but apparently his thumb is not working well enough. In the middle of winter, his electricity gets cut off. The bill is enormous. I use all my confirmation money to pay it. When I tell him, I'm sure that he'll be happy, that he'll throw his arms around me, thank me, and be grateful that he doesn't need to freeze because his child is coming to visit.

But he's not happy. He gets angry, saying that he would much rather have used the money for something else. He leaves enraged, borrows some money from a friend, and gets drunk. He won't be able to pay me back.

My parents are worried. They tell me they don't understand. "He's so much older than you," they say. "What do you talk about?"

"All sorts of things," I reply.

THE TRUTH IS, I don't remember our conversations. Not a single one. I remember things that I said, that he said, but only fragments. Words must have been less important to me then. It must have been the sex. Sex must have been important.

I remember I was very happy, that he made me incredibly happy and incredibly desperate at the same time. Maybe that's just what it's like to be sixteen? Maybe life would have been like that regardless? Maybe the gaping chasm between me and my classmates who resisted alcohol and did their homework every day would have been just as wide? Maybe I confused love and hormones? It's possible.

When I heard that he was dead, I tried to unravel our story. It was impossible. I could only remember one version—how we met and how we split—but the words that made up the narrative were gone. He moved on, lived in another town, and had more children and more girlfriends. Those who knew him said he was always beautiful, right until the very end.

If I'd heard about his death when it happened, I would have gone to his funeral. I was living an altogether different life in Oslo. I had met A. We were married. I had walked down the aisle with my father, my hands trembling as I held a bouquet of white orchids. I had done something that had surprised both A and myself: I had said yes in a voice that also trembled slightly. I had become a mother. I had used so many words in my life, written so many books. With my first real boyfriend, words had obviously not been that important.

I was only told about his death by an acquaintance, long after the fact. At first, it didn't seem to have anything to do with me. Only later did I realize that I had been wrong.

I feel immense relief at leaving him. I'm only going to university to study and will come back on the weekends, I say, but I know that I won't. I know that he needs me in his own way and I know that I'm finished with him. I won't come back. I'll come back to the mountains, to the sea, to the cobbled main street in the city centre — just not to him.

He writes me some letters that arrive in the mailbox at my new apartment. He must have got my address from Mom. It's probably the first and only time that he has contacted her. His letters are never long, but it's obvious that he has put enormous effort into them. He mixes small and capital letters and his writing is child-like. He writes things that he would often not be able to say when he's sober: I love you; I can't live without you. The paper smells of rolling tobacco. The letters smell of him and it's a smell I no longer like, a smell I don't want to acknowledge. The girl I share the apartment with finds the letters on my desk. She's older than me and is studying literature. I look up to her.

"Who is he?" she asks, and I see the laughter bubbling under the surface.

"My little brother," I say quickly.

"Wow, how old is he?"

"Ten," I reply. "He's ten."

As a student, I felt that I was sexually experienced. I felt old but still tried out different things for the sake of appearances. I had sex hanging from a rafter in a loft, for example. Obviously, it was quite a strain to hang there, but once I realized that my fellow conspirator thought that I was huffing and puffing because it felt good, I stopped putting it on and kept going. Afterwards I claimed that I'd come and that it had been fantastic. I had sex in public toilets, in cleaning cupboards, and behind bushes in the park. I twisted and turned and moaned. I was pretty convincing.

Once I had sex with a stranger in an elevator. He played in a band and had a tattoo on his chest that read *I'm the Sinking Ship*. I pondered its meaning as I faked an orgasm. I came to the conclusion that he must see himself as some kind of catastrophe, and that I should abandon my post. But I stayed, mainly because he stopped the elevator between the third and fourth floors, and also because I felt obliged: both to stay and to fake. Why did I do it?

I knew that in all likelihood I would never see him again, but I still made the effort. It's possible that kind of sex relies on some sort of contract: men can't deal with being losers.

I've also suffered from unrequited love. He didn't want me the way I wanted him, but then one evening he took me home with him all the same. He stroked my hair and said things he didn't mean. After we'd slept together, I told everyone he was terrible in bed. He was mortified and desperate, and begged to have another chance to do better. He couldn't have that reputation hanging over him. It made me feel great to discover how much damage I could do with such a careless comment.

AS A STUDENT, I soon start a quasi-relationship with a boy. He's a year older than me and is always happy. I love it initially. He wants to come home with me and meet my parents. He introduces me to his circle of friends, which is big. He makes mix tapes of his favourite music for me—music that he wants me to like, too. He calls them "love tapes." When we have sex, I pretend to come before he does. At first he is proud of his skills, that he can make me come so fast, but after a while he starts to get worried and wonders if I'm a nymphomaniac. So I take it down a notch, since I don't want to appear to be *too* horny.

He starts to get on my nerves very quickly. I develop an interest in one of his friends instead. He's older and not good-looking. He looks as though he doesn't care about his clothes or appearance. He lives in a tumble-down tenement behind the train station, without a shower or bath, only a freezing toilet in the stairwell.

He seems to be unhappy. He has a record collection that I come to love and thick glasses that make him look smarter than he is. He doesn't look like someone who's likely to make "love tapes." It becomes evident fairly quickly that he doesn't want anything to do with me. His disinterest drives me insane. For him, it's unthink-able that he might get involved with his friend's girl-friend—some kind of code of honour, evidently. Still, I offer myself to him. I'm pretty sure he doesn't get many offers like that, but he says no.

"You're one of those people who wants what they can't have," he says. Of course he's right, but I don't tell him.

"No, I'm not like that. You're wrong," I say.

His guitar is the best thing about him, along with the fact that he writes his own songs. His lyrics are subtle, both funny and serious at the same time. I ask him to play his songs over and over again. At night, I climb through his window when he's asleep. I'm convinced he'll be happy when he wakes up and sees me there, and eventually give in. But he's not happy, nor does he give in.

He's a hard cookie. I don't exactly break him, but I wear him down, day by day. I am persistent in my pursuit. I want to know why he's so unhappy.

He cries the first time we have sex. I pretend to have a pretty good orgasm, even though he suffers from premature ejaculation.

"If you leave me now, I'll kill you," he says, before falling asleep.

We're lying on the hard sofa bed in his condemned flat. It feels soft; it feels right. I assure him that I'm not going anywhere. I don't believe a word I say. He won't kill me if I leave him.

Soon he's forgotten to distrust me. I notice that he looks at me with a kind of intensity, almost love.

One morning after we've got out of bed and are sitting together under a blanket, smoking cigarettes, and listening to records, he tells me that he loves me. Well, he doesn't say those exact words. I say I need to hear "I Want You" by Elvis Costello, and he says, "Do it yourself," which surprises me because he normally doesn't like anyone else touching his records. They're the only possessions he really cares about. He lifts them gently, as you would a baby, and strokes the covers. He hardly shows me as much care, but now he's saying, "Do it yourself."

I draw the record out of its cover by the edges as he watches me. I put it down on the turntable and feel his eyes burning on my neck. I lift the needle and just as I'm about to let go, he says: "If you get it right, I love you."

I hit just the right groove, and an expectant, crackling silence fills the room. Precision is not usually my thing, but I've hit the spot and he loves me. It's the first time he says it.

And immediately the spell is broken. I don't love him. I almost can't stand him. It was the chase that thrilled me, the act of breaking him down. Now there's nothing but a bad conscience. I have to find a way to extract myself from the relationship, but how?

I sleep with someone else the next day. He's a social worker. It's very easy to relate to him. Maybe it's because his job is to be relatable. Afterwards, I creep in through my boyfriend's window and tell him what I've done. His face reveals nothing. I realize that I don't really know him, and I have no idea what he is capable of doing.

We sleep together on the sofa bed. It's me who cries as the dawn approaches and the day forces its way in through the curtains; it's me who has regrets. He regrets nothing. I continue to be horrible, and every night I throw stones at his window and sleep in his bed. I cry. He comforts me. I pretend to have great, dramatic orgasms.

"I want to feel that I'm alive," I say one evening.

It's September now, but the days are still warm. The new semester has started at university. The trees are still green. It rains less than usual. The punch is unexpected. My lip splits, my nose bleeds.

"Do you feel it now?" he asks, and wipes the blood from his fist on the pillow.

"Yes, I think so," I say.

He doesn't apologize.

After that, there is always a hint of scorn in his face whenever he looks at me, a kind of contempt, almost like he's saying *can't you see how pathetic you are?*

Many years later, I'm in Trondheim for work. I've heard from some friends that he's moved there, like a lot of his friends did when they finished university. Some of them turn up to hear my talk. They fall silent when I ask about him.

Some weeks later, I walk past his old apartment. The building has been demolished without a trace. Everything has vanished: the windowpanes that I threw stones at in the dark, the sofa bed I slept on, his record collection. It's all gone.

LUDMILA IS EMPTYING the dishwasher up in the kitchen. She's making a terrible racket with the china. I can't help thinking that a lot of the plates have been chipped recently, and it's obvious why. Can't she just be a little more careful? I try to concentrate on a talk by a Dr. Rauch that I've come across on the Internet.

She talks about women who can achieve orgasms from the tiniest things. One woman, for example, can't brush her teeth without coming. She's tried to change toothpaste, but it doesn't help. It's the movement itself that triggers the orgasm. You would think the woman has "excellent dental hygiene," as Dr. Rauch puts it, but instead she believes she is possessed by demons and has started to use mouthwash. Another woman can reach orgasm simply by deciding to. Dr. Rauch interviewed her in a sushi restaurant, and asked whether she could come right then and there.

"Of course," the woman replied, "but if it's all right, I'd rather finish my food first."

She did it on a park bench afterwards—and it only took a minute.

Dr. Rauch explains that dead people can also have orgasms. Not corpses, of course, but people who are brain-dead and being kept alive on life support. They can have an orgasm if they are stimulated at a certain point on their spine.

"Of course it's not always as good," Dr. Rauch says, "but an orgasm is an orgasm."

It's insulting that even brain-dead people can achieve something that I can't. It's downright depressing.

I decide to donate my organs. If I can't succeed now when I'm alive, I might be luckier when my brain dies. I download the donor app from the App Store. It can't do any harm, I think, and I paradoxically feel closer to my goal than I have for a long time.

I GO TO TEL Aviv to study. I'm going to write about the influence of Zionism in literature after the Second World War. When I arrive, I discover that the professor who is supposed to be my supervisor has gone away for two months.

Suddenly I have nothing to do, and my apartment in Norway has already been rented out. No one is waiting for me at home, either. What should I do? I stay.

It's January and cold. I book myself into a hostel on Ben Yehuda Street. It's freezing at night, but the sun warms up during the day and I forget to buy a blanket. I meet the Englishman at the hostel. He's a soldier who was injured during the Falklands War. All he has to show for his time in the army is a pile of meaningless photographs that have gotten stuck together. He works as a tiler in Ramat Gan and Beer Sheva during the week.

We sleep together the first evening we meet in the dining room. It feels natural, not dangerous. I think he is big and stupid — so big that he can protect me from everything I believe is threatening in this new world. In a way, it is he who is dangerous, but I don't realize that yet. I think I can deal with someone like him. He's a simple sentimentalist, but over the course of a few weeks, I become utterly dependent on him. I start to scream at him when he doesn't come home at night.

"Where have you been?" I shout. "Where have you been?!"

I ask even though I know he'd got himself a room at the Green House for the night with a Danish girl he used to see.

"Shush...shush. Nothing happened, baby."

He strokes my hair like a loving father. He's lying, but his hands soothe me. I have no pride. The only thing that matters is that he's come back.

He is pathologically jealous himself. I can't talk to anyone without consequences. I don't know who he's going to hit: me or the man I'm talking to. I learn to look over my shoulder, to always have him in the corner of my eye, so I can see what he sees. It's worse when there are Norwegians or Swedes around, because then he doesn't understand what we're saying, and that sends him into a rage and makes him unpredictable. One day I'm talking to a Swedish boy that I have absolutely no interest in — I'm telling him where it's easy to get a job and how to go about it — and get an ashtray to the head.

The Swedish boy gives me a look because he doesn't understand.

I get three stitches at the emergency room, which is nothing.

He's so upset. It will never happen again, he promises. He'll do anything if I let him stay. His eyes are so icy blue. His voice quivers. It doesn't matter whether or not I believe him, because I've granted his wish.

I feel sorry for him. I keep telling myself that our relationship is just temporary; it won't last. He's so much older than me and different from me. Once upon a time, his family was rich, but then his father lost the factory and everything was gone in an instant: the house with the swimming pool, the private school, the dog—his father shot it in the garden when he heard the news. He never told me what the factory produced or why his father lost it. Sometimes I think it's all just a lie.

He signed up for the army after that and became a paratrooper. He says this in a voice that tells me it's worthy of respect.

Parts of his left thigh are missing. At first he tells me a crocodile bit him when he was stationed in Belize, but later I find out it was an accident: he got caught under a trailer and was in hospital for six months.

He's an Israeli citizen because he was married to an Israeli woman. The accident happened while they were living in England. She wasn't happy there—didn't like the climate or the people and got even thinner than she already was. She worked in a pub and did her job well. People liked her, but it didn't help. She left, returning to the sun and desert. He ended up under a trailer and in a hospital bed for six months.

When he finally got down to Israel, so much had changed. She didn't love him anymore, but he stayed all the same. There was nothing for him in England; there was nothing for him in Israel either, but still he stayed.

THE CITY IS hard to understand. Men search me with metal detectors in the supermarket, run their hands over my breasts and around my waist. It's their job, they say, with a sheepish smile.

There are beautiful young women in the streets with machine guns slung over their shoulders. People are direct, verging on impolite. Men shout at me regularly. Some think I'm a Russian prostitute and ask me how much I cost. It's not necessarily because I'm scantily dressed, but because I look Russian and there are so many Russian prostitutes here.

The streets smell of exhaust and spices. The traffic is as temperamental as the people. After three days, I get a job in a pub.

"Come tomorrow at nine o'clock," the man behind the bar tells me, when I ask if they've got any jobs.

I'm put behind the bar at nine o'clock the next day. The man leaves, and I have a job. I work from nine to nine. The clientele is largely English construction workers with contracts all over the country. My first customer orders a coffee. I make a cup of instant coffee and my long hair falls into the cup that I'm about to serve him.

"Get your fucking hair out of my coffee," he says.

I try to excuse myself by explaining that I've just washed my hair. When I ask how my shampoo tastes, he laughs and gives me a two-shekel tip.

The UN soldiers come pouring in on the weekend and I'm not prepared. They want drinks. It's possible they have a lot to forget. I can't make anything other than tequilas, and they seem happy with that. They down the drinks and try to fondle my tits.

I have to find out how things work for myself. It takes me a little less than a week to master the coffee machine. I'm not familiar with anything other than filtered coffee and instant with or without milk. The possibilities are endless here. I also have to teach myself how to make cocktails. Tequila will not satisfy everyone.

I find an English bookshop on Bograshov where I read a book about making cocktails. I start to get by after two weeks, but it's a long time before I can match Sally. She's American and works in the evenings. She's blonde and quick. The Israelis love her.

I go downtown when I have time off. It's ugly-beautiful: the colourful fountain by Dizengoff, the movie theatre where I see *Schindler's List* in the midst of an uncontrollably sobbing audience, Carmel Market with its cackling hens and exotic fruits, and the endless beach that stretches as far as the eye can see.

The hostel is occupied by a collection of more or less permanent guests, the majority of whom are young travellers looking for short- and long-term work in Tel Aviv.

Barbara has brought her son with her from the States, so that he can fight for the Cause. It's not his cause, but he does what he's told. He puts on the green, newly ironed uniform every day, just as his mother wants him to, just as he thinks his grandparents would have wanted him to had they not died in Dachau. He does what he believes is best, but it's people like him who don't let the city forget, who don't allow peace. One night someone pisses on his gun, which is stored in the hostel safe. The two Englishmen responsible don't know that they could go to prison for ruining a military gun. They do it "just for a laugh." Two men in uniform come to get Brandon, one of the Englishmen. We never see him again.

Then there's Sonja. Sonja is so beautiful when she smiles, but she never does because she's angry. She carries an enormous burden of guilt for what Germany, her country, has done to the Jews. She sold everything she owned in Hamburg to move here. She is twenty-three. She's now learning Hebrew and intends to stay here. It helps, she says. It helps ease the guilt.

If anyone criticizes Israel's role in the conflict, she goes lobster red right down to the roots of her fair hair. I've never seen anyone get so red. She doesn't speak much English and doesn't have the vocabulary to defend her new homeland. When Israeli men try to bed her, she doesn't dare say no; it's part of her penance to let them do what they want with her.

I WORK FIVE days a week, without ever becoming a good barmaid. It's not for me. My hands shake, my hair dips in the coffee, and I stand on people's toes. The pay isn't great, but I learn to play darts well and earn more money that way. There's a competition every day at lunch with each person putting ten shekels in the pot. Some days I go home with two hundred shekels in my pocket.

I love coming home at the end of a working day. The others who work dayshifts are already there. The men sit and drink lukewarm beer in their work clothes. The room smells of sweat and cement, and the small kitchen is full of Romanians frying mushrooms and pork. Sometimes we go down to the beach for a swim, other times we just sit there, play cards, chat, and drink until we fall into our beds. I love the hostel and the people in it, where me and a handful of others make up a stable core amid everything that is changing. We're like a family. It's safe and comfortable. We look down on the people who are here on holiday. What do they know about how it all fits together?

One day a mother turns up with her daughter, who is my age. They're from Washington and on a world tour together. They treat each other like friends. In the morning they visit museums and go shopping; in the evening they sit at a table in the corner of the bar, where they drink tea and play Trivial Pursuit. It looks nice. I find myself missing my mother, even though we're not friends and we're not travelling the world together and drinking tea and playing Trivial Pursuit.

I talk to the mother one evening when the Englishman isn't there. She asks about the city and the country. I answer as best I can. Then, without warning, she asks, "What are you doing with *him*?"

I'm perplexed and don't know how to answer. Is it any of her business?

Before I can say anything, she apologizes.

"It's just, I'm a mother to a girl your age, and he is…"

I hold up my hand to show that I understand what she means. I feel the need to show her that I'm in control, that I know exactly what I'm doing.

"I can go home whenever I want. I'm going to go back to university. We've got nothing in common. He's a tiler.

Do you think I don't know that we've got no future? I'm just having a bit of fun. Surely that's allowed?"

I don't know where the words come from. I'm not telling the truth. I can't just leave; I'm not in control.

"That's not quite what I meant," the mother says quietly.

"Like I said, I just want to have fun," I say, with false conviction.

When I turn around, he's standing behind me. I don't know how long he's been there or how much he's heard. Shame burns my cheeks. What have I said? What have I said that he might have heard?

He's going to hit me. If he heard what I said, he'll hit me.

But he doesn't hit me. When the evening is done, he lies down beside me and tells me that he loves more than anything else in the world. Then I know that he's heard everything. The shame eats me up.

ONE EVENING WHEN I come home, my belongings are in two plastic bags by the reception desk. No one can look me in the eye. Sean from New Zealand, who works at the hostel, explains that he got orders from management to throw me out. I look him in the eye and he shakes his head, suggesting that he has no choice. I immediately know that it's got something to do with the Englishman.

"He went berserk here today. Sorry…"

"What did he do?"

"He floored the little Dutchman in number ten; he's okay, though. And some glasses were broken. It's nothing major, but you know, it's not exactly pleasant for the other guests."

"But *I* didn't go berserk. We're not married. You don't have the right to throw *me* out!"

Sean shrugs.

"If you're here, he'll come back, you know that. And we don't want him here."

Sean hands me an envelope with an address. I go there, even though I don't want to.

I take a number ten bus, along the shore to Jaffa, the old part of the city. I can see the Turkish clock tower in the distance.

We live in a straw hut on the roof of a hostel. It's too hot to sleep inside at night but too cold to sleep outside in the morning. Through the gap between the wall and the roof, you can see down to the bazaar with its colourful offerings of carpets and jewels. There are cars, horses and carts, loud men who drink black tea and play *shesh besh*. Shouting voices are constant, frenetic, as though there was always something at stake. The quarter was built by the Turks and is not like any other part of Tel Aviv. This is an Arab area with an Arab bakery that sells bagels with sesame seeds and cheese from Bulgaria.

There's a derelict casino down by the beach. I don't know who organizes it, but we're given permission to move in. The roulette table is our dining table, and we sleep on mattresses on the floor. We buy a television. I lie there when the Englishman is at work laying tiles. He comes home covered in a film of white dust. It hangs on his eyelashes and in his hair. We swim every afternoon. He lies in the waves and the white dust rinses away.

The golden sand and Mediterranean are no more than a stone's throw from the casino. The Arabic fishermen watch us with lowered eyes. No one has it better than we do. I think they're jealous of us, but the Englishman says they're staring at us because they don't like us. Sometimes when I'm alone on the beach, men lie behind the sand dunes and masturbate while they watch me. The strange thing is they don't seem to be ashamed. If I send them an icy look, they just smile, like proud children who have just learned to ride a bike. *Look at me, Mommy! Look what I can do!*

It seldom bothers me, but I don't understand it. One day I tell the Englishman. He flies into a rage — screams and lashes out — and throws whatever he has in his hands. He wants me to go downtown with him and point out any culprits. I tell him that's impossible, since I don't know many Arabs. They all look the same to me. I'm so glad that there are no longer any witnesses to his abuse. I think I can live with it as long as no one else knows. I'm ashamed of his temper. He's so unpredict-able and so irrational, but he can't see it himself. He isn't embarrassed.

I feel ashamed about so many things. I can't relax. I can't come.

I WORK AS a waitress at christenings and bar mitz-vahs. I learn to prepare hummus, *börek*, and egg-plant. I always feel like an outsider. The families are big and exude energy. They throw the babies up in the air and sometimes call out: sixty kilos of meat for this four-kilo baby. Help yourselves!

They dance, they shout. They know that any day might be their last because things can happen, bombs can explode. I miss my own family. But I long to belong where I am, even more than I miss them.

I later read that others have also felt the same need to belong when they've lived with these people. Their tragedy, their blood, unites them: it's something you can get close to, but never be part of—and that makes the need to belong even stronger. I want to be part of it; I want to belong; I yearn for their tragedy, but it's not mine, and never can be. Why am I not grateful for that?

On Holocaust Day, traffic stands still for a minute.

The exhaust swirls up into the shimmering air and evaporates. A siren sounds. Then the cars start to move again. There is no dancing that day. Or, there is not *supposed* to be any dancing that day.

Some people dance all the same, the ones who share blood, but not the tragedy. Some of the Jews from Yemen or Morocco say there's no want of tragedies, but the Holocaust was quite a while ago now, so what about us? What about our tragedies? The new translation of the Haggadah says: *In every generation, a person is obligated to view himself as if he were the one who left Egypt.* Is that true? I want to be someone who fights, someone who is forced to fight all the time.

Morning on the beach is my favourite time of day. Everyone else is at work and I have the warm sand to myself. It's around this time that I start to write. No matter where I go, I always have a notebook with me. The language is mine alone. Sometimes I feel that I'm losing it, that it's drowning and disappearing in all the other languages. My language is spoken by so few, and I have to protect it.

At first I just take notes about my many arguments with the Englishman and when he hits me, but gradually the sentences get longer and sometimes I can't stop. But I always have to be alone. If anyone sees me writing, everything retreats back inside, like the bubbles in a pan of boiling water pulled off the heat. My words scurry back to where they came from. I'm not ashamed of writing, but I have to be alone. Writing is something private.

And that's the way it will always be for me. Many years later, after my seventh novel, a doctor asks me what I write about while taking my blood pressure. It's only small talk, but my blood pressure rockets. The doctor looks worried. I tell him to measure it again, without asking me about my writing.

He does as I ask.

My blood pressure is completely normal.

"What are you writing?" a voice asks me in an Australian accent. I put my hands over the book to protect the pages and bury it in the golden sand.

"Nothing."

"Oh well."

He doesn't ask any more about it, which I like. Instead, he holds out his hand and introduces himself. "Jed."

I do the same. "Julie."

"We need some extras for a film we're making and they're not supposed to look like typical Israelis since it's an American film. They're shooting here because it's cheaper."

"What's the film?"

"Don't ask me. I just make the coffee."

There's something bright and carefree about him.

I follow him along the beach and we walk all the way

into Tel Aviv, stopping outside one of the beach bars. It's a hive of activity. A middle-aged woman is handing out sandwiches to all the extras, who are wearing seventies clothing. In the roasting sun, makeup artists are skipping around with powder puffs and an actor I recognize is reading through his lines. I can't remember any films he's been in, and when I turn around to ask Jed, he's gone and I'm not sure what to do with myself until a woman comes over and pulls me into the costume room behind the bar. "Pick something that fits," she says.

The film is about Uri Geller, the magician, and my first task is to dance in a packed bar, without music, while the actor I recognize whispers his lines into the ear of a beautiful female actress.

"You should have brought the boys!"

"No, they're into classical!"

We do thirteen takes before we're finished. Then it's time for lunch. We sit down in the shade and are given sandwiches by a smiling Jed, who talks to everyone. He's got long, blond hair and is tanned and bare-chested. He looks like a surfer.

After lunch, we sit in the audience at an American TV show where Uri Geller is a guest, bending his spoons. We clap. Jed's in the audience, too. He's wearing a shirt that makes him look silly, and he strokes his hand over my thigh as the camera rolls. I struggle to concentrate on Uri Geller and the spoons.

Jed wants me to go home with him.

I imagine what the Englishman's face would look like if I didn't come home. What would he do? He's stayed out himself. He's checked into the Green House with his old girlfriend. Why can't I do the same? A sense of defiance starts to grow. Why can't I do what I want? Am I scared?

We go out into the stark sunlight and Jed continues to stroke me. His touch is intoxicating. Any fear of what might happen disappears and is banished by the sun, sand, and Jed's light laughter. Everything seems so simple. Jed says he's borrowing an apartment. I hear myself saying "Why not?" and I am suddenly sitting in a taxi, deciding to take it one day at a time.

I'M WOKEN BY unknown voices speaking very fast Hebrew. The voices are softer than the ones I'm used to from the bazaar. They snigger. Jed is lying beside me. He's kicked off the sheet and is sleeping naked like a log. I see the camera crew right in front of us. They've got microphones, spotlights, and are standing at the end of the bed looking at us. I nudge Jed. He turns over on his side and pulls up the sheet.

I snatch back the sheet and push him so hard that he falls out of bed.

"Good morning, Jed," says the cameraman.

I look at Jed desperately, as he gets up from the floor. His fair hair is sticking out in every direction. I wait for him to get angry and turf out the camera crew, but he doesn't. He just smiles and says "good morning" back, as he hops around on one leg, pulling on his pants.

Our audience claps and I look around for my clothes. It takes a while before it all makes sense.

"We're filming a sitcom, but this is much better than the script," says the guy who is presumably the director.

I look at Jed askance.

He explains sheepishly that this is the set of a sitcom and that he also makes the coffee here and does whatever work is needed in return for accommodation.

"Can I have cup of coffee?" the cameraman asks, and everyone laughs.

I pull the sheet and my clothes with me into the bathroom. The tone outside is relaxed and easy. By now the Englishman will no doubt be raging—and possibly scared, but mostly raging. I feel a resistance to the idea of going back to the casino; I want to stay here with Jed in all the light and embarrassment. Do I have to go back?

Yes, I have to go back. I can't keep putting it off.

I try to steel myself in the taxi, making up lies that are as watertight as possible. I rehearse my lines, even though I know it's pointless.

O NE DAY I come home from working at a bar
mitzvah, and the backyard is full of people. The
ground is covered in golden sand, and there are coloured
lights strung up in the trees and between the build-
ings. There's even a camel — a real one. Techno music
is thumping out of some enormous loudspeakers. Two
men stop me to say that I'm not dressed well enough
to get in. I try to explain that I live here and point to
the fire exit behind them. Eventually they let me pass,
albeit somewhat reluctantly.

No one at the casino can explain what's happened.
Some cars just turned up with sand and a camel. It's
making the Arabs in the liquor store on the corner
desperate.

"That's where the electricity for everything is coming from," explains Norman, a South African who has
moved in with us.

"But surely they're paying?"

Norman shakes his head.

"But who *are* they?"

"Mafia. They do what they like. We'll just have to hope they leave."

But they don't leave. The music thumps every night. It starts around ten in the evening and goes until five in the morning. People dance and drink. And we have to drink too, if we're going to sleep at all. We eat to the music, make love to the music, and throw up to the music. Even though it's July and the Mediterranean is right outside our window, we are aggressive and pale. *Thump, thump, thump.* There's no point in going anywhere else. It's as though our bodies' defence systems switch to receive, and we hear the thumping even when it's not there, even when the monster loudspeakers are empty and silent, even when the sand is stripped of dancing bodies and only the camel stands in the sand, ruminating. Jesus, it's a wonder that the camel is still alive.

I have no choice. I have to leave.

I get onto the bus in the same way that a foal breaks free from its tether. The sense of freedom is overwhelming, but at the same time, I'm exhausted. I've told him I'll be back in three weeks. It's a lie. I'm never coming back.

"I'll wait for you," he says.

"Good," I reply.

THE TECHNO MUSIC thumps in my head long after I'm back in Norway. I stay in a cabin that belongs to one of my uncles. The pine forest surrounds it like a great wall. There is barely a sound outside, but my body pulses to the music, it won't let me go. I cry and sleep. In the autumn, I go back to university.

It's hard to accept normal life again. I can't sit still in lectures. I receive a thick envelope in the mail that contains all the letters I've written to the Englishman. On a piece of green paper it says: *The light within a woman's eyes that lies and lies and lies and lies.*

He phones me a few times after sending the note. He's furious. I say nothing. He's so far away. Nothing he shouts into the receiver will make me do anything other than what I'm doing. The dreams only start when he stops calling. I dream that he turns up at my lectures or sits on the stairs outside my apartment and waits. He's angry. In one of the dreams, I have a husband and children. He wants to kill them.

I don't know it yet, but these dreams will plague me for a long time. They don't just pass.

Many years later, a Dutch woman calls me. She's had a child with the Englishman, and phones to find out if he's always been like *this*. I ask what she means by *this*, but it's just to win some time. I know perfectly well what she's asking.

"Possessive, jealous, violent," she says. "I'm always

being compared to you. He still has some photos of you in his wallet. You're naked in one of them. Is it true that you've written a book about him?"

I tell her that it's not about him at all, and that, no, it hasn't been translated into Dutch. My husband's family is visiting. Alva is asleep. The phone call makes me uneasy.

"I don't know what to do," she says.

"I'm afraid I can't help you," I say, and put down the receiver without saying goodbye.

Some time passes and then I realize that the dreams have stopped. They belong to someone else now.

I find out that he's died the same way that I found out that my first boyfriend died: by chance. But's it's through Facebook this time. One of the South Africans tells me during a chat: *Didn't you know? He died two years ago.* And I say that I didn't know, just as I had said once before.

Am I ashamed about Israel? I kissed men and women. Am I ashamed? If I didn't come then, why should I come now? Is it because deep down I believe that an orgasm is something too private to share with others?

My stomach feels empty and my vagina is sore. There's no flatbread left. The zucchini has been eaten. The baby oil is almost empty.

THE TELEPHONE RINGS, but I try to ignore it. Mr. Rabbit is working hard and I have to focus on what I'm here for. The tickling feeling in my legs is back. I'm going to come; I can feel that it's not long now. It will happen soon — at any moment. But the telephone doesn't stop; it just keeps ringing and ringing.

So I pick it up.

"Hello?"

"Are you coming this evening or what?"

"Sorry?"

I throw the vibrator aside. Pure reflex.

"We're going to see a movie, aren't we?"

Suddenly I remember that I'd arranged to go the movie theatre with Vibeke to see a documentary about some guy from Detroit who never managed to break through with his music in the seventies, but then discovers that he's a superstar in South Africa, having spent years working in a factory in the U.S. Vibeke has called to ask if I'm coming. Couldn't she have put it another way? I get irritated.

"I'm not sure that I can make it," I say.

"But we agreed. I've booked two tickets!"

Of course she's booked two tickets. Vibeke is always so officious and organizes things that don't require advance planning.

"We're counting on you. And everyone else is coming…"

"Yes, yes, I'm sure everyone else is coming!"

"Sorry?"

"I'm working on it, I said."

I hang up. My arm aches, but I haven't thought of giving up. For some reason, Michael's face appears when I close my eyes. It's as though his amber eyes are following my hands.

ONCE I'D MADE the decision to get an au pair, I realized we would need to get someone to build a bed platform where she could sleep. A is good with his hands, but he never finishes anything: our walls were left without skirting boards for years and things never got painted. If anything was going to happen, we had to hire someone, but I didn't know any handymen. I needed someone to install the TV cable and to do some other electrical work, and of course, a carpenter to build the platform. The Yellow Pages were full of carpenters and electricians, but I had no idea if these people were any good. The only thing I could do was wait until A had time to find someone.

I GOT MARTIN ready. He was going to sleep outside in the stroller; he was tired and wriggled a lot, crying at the smallest thing. When I finally got him out the door,

I had to force him down into the stroller and strap him in, but he fell asleep almost instantly. It was crisp and dry outside; everything was yellow and blue. There were three Polish workers painting the outside of the neighbouring house. The whole place was being renovated. I stopped and rocked the stroller with my right hand, which I do out of habit even when Martin is fast asleep. The labourers looked at me expectantly.

"Do you need any extra work?"

"What kind of work?" the smallest and best-looking of them asked.

All three were wearing white overalls that were no longer that colour, with an advertisement for Beckers, the decorators, splashed on the back.

"I need to build a . . ." I couldn't think of what to call it. I didn't even know if there was a proper word for it.

"A sleeping platform," I ventured.

"Ah, a sleeping platform," the good-looking one repeated. He said something to his colleagues in Polish and they nodded, in cahoots.

"And I need someone for . . . electrics."

They laughed.

"Yes, we can help you."

I explained that I lived in the neighbouring house and that they could come see the room when they had time. They nodded, saying it would have to be in the evening, since they worked until ten. They also asked if it would be possible to build the sleeping platform on Sunday because that was the only time they were free. The slight, good-looking one did all the talking. He had amazingly light brown, almost yellow, eyes under a dark fringe. He told me that they worked for a Norwegian company that had given them a permanent contract. They nodded proudly. If the company found out that they were taking jobs on the side, they would no doubt be fired, so they would have to be discreet. The company only paid 75 kroner an hour, so it was tempting to take on extra work when the opportunity arose.

I promised to be as discreet as possible. I thought that I would give them 150 kroner an hour, at least. 75 kroner! That was scandalous.

"Julie," I said, introducing myself. I held out my hand.

"Michael," he said, as he shook it. His hand was cold and rough.

They came to look at the room that very same evening. It was almost half past ten. When they rang the bell, A was sitting in his boxer shorts as usual, eating flatbread and drinking milk. It was something he'd done since he was a child, and I can't stand the habit. I got great pleasure from the fact that they came in and saw him like that. Perhaps I just imagined it, but he seemed a little peeved, or embarrassed, when the Poles tramped through the living room into the study. I made drawings and explained. Michael's yellow eyes followed my gesticulating hands. It wouldn't take more than one Sunday, he assured me. They only had to do a few things and could get the materials cheap, which would suit us all. He was right, of course.

"Shouldn't we wait a little?" A asked, after I had shown the Poles out.

"Wait? What's the point in waiting? She has to have somewhere to sleep."

"Who?"

"Ludmila," I snapped.

A was barely interested in the person who would change my life for the better. Typical! Or perhaps it wasn't so strange. He would still get his food on the table — there would still be no need for him to wash the floor or tidy up after the children. I didn't say anything. It wouldn't be long now until everything was different.

"But couldn't she have the room as it is?"

"No, I don't think so. It's important that she likes it here. I'm going to have a little living room made up for her downstairs, so she doesn't have to be on top of us."

"I see. I still think we should wait. How much is all this going to cost?"

"Don't think about it."

A made it sound like I was doing this for my own sake. I had enough money saved to get the sleeping platform made. And anyway, I saw it as an investment. The

MICHAEL CAME ON the Sunday, as agreed. When the doorbell rang at seven in the morning, I didn't realize who it was at first. I had just finished breastfeeding Martin and put him back in his crib. Alva was still asleep, miraculously, and Liva had not woken up yet. All was well with the world. Then I remembered the Poles. I put on my bathrobe and went to open the door. I wanted to ask A to let them in, but he was asleep and had already made it clear that this was my project.

THEY WERE WEARING overalls, with tool box in hand. Michael had a stepladder under his arm. His yellow eyes looked me up and down as I stood there in my bathrobe. I hadn't shaved my legs, and Michael noticed. I was sure he noticed.

I moved to one side to indicate that they could come in. I should have asked if they wanted a cup of coffee, but I couldn't face making it, so instead disappeared down into the bedroom to try to get some more sleep. Martin had still not woken up, and A was still snoring, of course. Just as I got down the stairs, I heard Alva screaming at the top of her lungs. I ran up the stairs again and saw one of the Poles standing petrified in the hallway.

"I thought toilet," he explained.

I gently opened the door to Alva's room.

"There, there, it's all right, Mommy's here," I comforted her.

I pointed to the toilet door on the other side of the hall and watched the Pole slunk in with his tail between his legs.

"I thought he was a robber," Alva sobbed. "A nasty robber."

"We've talked about this before. There are no robbers here. The nice man just wants to help us make a room ready for Ludmila."

"Who's Mila?"

"She's going to come and live with us."

"Why?"

"She's going to help us look after Martin and keep the house tidy. She's called an *au pair*."

Alva repeated the word and tested it out.

"Vilde has an au pair—and a dog!"

"Yes, that's right. Vilde has an au pair."

"And a dog!"

"Yes, and a dog, too."

I of course wanted to mention that an au pair was a person and a dog was an animal, but I wasn't sure there was any point.

I HEAR A coming home upstairs and Alva and Liva tumble in with him. I normally meet them at the door, mostly because I'm dying for company. I hug them and ask questions about their day. I can just imagine them now, standing in the hallway listening, looking around, waiting for me. They look at their father and ask where I am. He doesn't know any more than they do. His feet are hesitant on the stairs.

"Julie? Are you here? What are you doing in there?"

He stands outside the bedroom door and rattles the handle. I can tell from his voice that he's annoyed. I turn off the vibrator.

"What's that noise?"

"What noise?"

"You're not using my beard trimmer on your bikini line again, are you?"

"No," I snap, and try to think of something to divert his attention.

"I've got a migraine," I say.

"When did you start getting migraines?"

"Does *when* matter?"

"No, it's just that I've never heard you talking about migraines before . . ."

"Well, I've got one today. Is that okay? Is it okay if I have a migraine for once, like everyone else? Can't you just leave me in peace?"

"Not everyone else gets migraines," A says.

I sigh. That's so typical.

"Are Ludmila and Martin out?"

"Yes," I reply.

"Should I fry some fish sticks?"

"Yes, why don't you fry some fish sticks!"

He can't fry anything other than fish sticks and eggs.

"Or I could scramble some eggs."

"Do what you like. I've got other things to focus on."

I lie in bed and get bored.

After a while, A knocks on the door and asks if my migraine feels better. A's really not so bad. I tell him that I'm feeling a lot better now. In fact, I continue, I'm so much better I can go to the shop now.

DAY 4

THE NUMBERS ON the clock radio flash 4:52. The day hasn't even started. A is snoring lightly and I can't sleep. My brain is churning. Before going to sleep, I read the extracts from Eva Braun's diary that were found after the war. When I got into bed, A tentatively stroked my back and I had to pretend that I was doing something important. I leafed demonstratively through Eva Braun's diary, which I had found on the Internet and printed out the week before. I didn't think I could tell A that I was masturbating full-time at the moment and was too sore to have any kind of sex. He probably wouldn't have understood.

Only a few pages of Eva Braun's diary were saved; the rest had been torn out. What would the world not give to read the missing pages?

Eva Braun knew Hitler in a way that no one else did. The missing diary would have told us a lot about him. As I think this rather ordinary thought, I have another extraordinary thought: *I'm going to complete Eva Braun's diary*. I'm going to pad out the scant twenty-two pages that end all too soon. I'm going to make her diary my own. My story will seamlessly merge with Eva's. Yes, Eva's, because we're on a first name basis now that we're going to be sharing our innermost thoughts and feelings. I creep out of bed and find the laptop on the kitchen table.

PROBLEM NUMBER ONE: I need a framing story. Maybe the missing pages from the diary could suddenly turn up at an auction? One of the neo-Nazi shops? It sounds feasible.

I'm ecstatic. This is what I've been longing for: the mother of all ideas. It doesn't matter what Eva and Hitler actually did in Munich, Berghof, and the bunker. I'm going to tell the story now.

I start with the most difficult aspect of the story: Why did Eva Braun love Hitler? When you read Eva Braun's slim diary, comprising twenty-two pages over a period of 113 days in 1935, it is quite clear that she did love him and she burned with jealousy; it was the man himself she wanted. Or perhaps it was his power that made him attractive. Hitler became chancellor in 1933 and was in Berlin the majority of the time. She seldom had him to herself, as is often the way with powerful men. I can feel myself getting angry that women with power are not attractive in the same way.

I wanted to write about Strindberg's *Miss Julie* to show how unfair it was that women are always presented as the losers. Miss Julie loses everything for a man who doesn't even have power, at least not in a political sense. Jean is powerful simply by being male. It is his sex alone that allows him to destroy Miss Julie, who is the daughter of a count.

When Eva Braun first saw Hitler, or when Hitler first saw Eva Braun, she was standing on a stepladder in Heinrich Hoffman's photography shop where she worked. Hoffman was Hitler's personal photographer. He made his fortune from all the portraits he took of the Führer that hung in every German home for the period that the madness lasted. When Hitler noticed Eva's lovely legs up the ladder, she was seventeen and he was forty. He was ten years younger than her father. It is said that Hitler liked young, agreeable girls—girls who let themselves be moulded. And Eva was such a girl, not to mention she was blonde and athletic. She was attractive, but not too beautiful, presumably intelligent, but not so much so that it was a problem. Perhaps Hitler wanted a path of least resistance? No one knows if they had sex. No one knows exactly what he wanted from her. But the miserly 2,000 words left in Eva's diary leave no doubt. She loved him to distraction. She was willing to die for him long before their final days in the bunker.

When the Americans reached Berghof on May 1, 1945, no one paid much attention to Eva Braun's home videos. They were stored away haphazardly, but contained good-quality colour images of SS generals sipping tea, women in summer dresses, a relaxed Hitler talking to women, dogs, and children. The films were not important to the Allies at the time, who were focused on finding evidence of war crimes to present at the Nuremberg trials. And in any case, the films were silent. They didn't prove anything. You couldn't even hear what Hitler was saying to the women and children or understand *how* he was saying it. No one had a good recording of Hitler's voice as it sounded in private, until a Finnish recording was found here in Norway a few years ago.

On June 4, 1942, Hitler travelled to Finland to wish Carl Gustaf Mannerheim, his ally, a happy birthday. The Finnish broadcasting company had somehow managed to plant a microphone in the train compartment where they were sitting and chatting. The voice that we hear has little in common with the demagogic voice of the people that urges the great masses to love the German empire and hate its enemies. It's actually quite ordinary. He praises the Russians for what they have achieved so far and does not condemn them as he would in public. The sentences are short. He pauses to think. He is relaxed and self-deprecating. It's not a voice you take an immediate dislike to, or associate with the Holocaust and genocide. It's the voice of an old uncle you don't see often enough.

I've seen a documentary about it all. With the help of the world's best dubbing artists and a new data program that registers lip movements and turns them into sound, it is possible to recreate Hitler's voice and bring the silent films to life.

The data program can also read what is said when the speaker is in profile, which is normally hard for most lip-readers.

The relationship between Eva Braun and Hitler becomes clearer: "You talk about a dress that doesn't fit you, imagine what my problems are like," Hitler says to Eva at a point where the war has turned and he might already know that he'll lose. In another clip he says in a tired but loving voice: "Why are you filming an old man like me? I should be filming you."

After the war had ended, the American military ordered Adolf Hitler's doctor to write a detailed medical report about him.

The documents show that Hitler was heavily medicated. The most astonishing detail is that his doctors gave him large quantities of cocaine, not for the high, but to treat his sore throat and blocked sinuses.

Hitler's biographers have concluded that he did not have an active sex life, but also that his best-known — and famously evil — doctor, Theodor Morell, gave him semen from young bulls to improve his waning potency. Morell's unconventional methods were highly controversial, and Hermann Göring called him *der Reichsspritzenmeister*. In one document, Morell talks about the relationship between Hitler and Eva Braun. Morell claims that Hitler did in fact have sex with Eva Braun, even though they normally slept in separate rooms.

The report also shows that Hitler took pills containing a poison called strychnine, which resulted in terrible stomach pains. Strychnine was supposed to strengthen the nervous system and was also seen as an aphrodisiac in traditional medicine. So it would appear that even if the Führer didn't have a sex drive, he did want one. But what about Eva? What did this bull-semen-drinking old man give her? The sex couldn't have been important to her. So maybe sex isn't the most important thing. I have to explore this idea, both for Eva's sake and my own.

I'm relieved. The idea of writing a modern version of Strindberg's *Miss Julie* has felt wrong for a long time and outdated somehow. I don't really remember what I thought was so brilliant about it. It must be the fact that, when I was at school, the play had touched me so much. It put me into a kind of trance. But why? Because I had the same name as the main character? Am I that simple? No, it was the idea of "the fall" — the idea that there was no way back — that attracted me to the book. It seemed so sad, but at the same time said so much about the unfairness of being a woman. Anna Karenina and Emma Bovary experience the same fate. You would have thought that those inequalities might have changed by now, but they're still present. What is so brilliant about the idea that the world doesn't change?

I WAS GIVEN an old edition of the play with black-and-white covers by an uncle on my eighteenth birthday. There was a hundred-kroner note inside the book, and on it he had written: *For our own Miss Julie.* Presumably the play aroused my interest because it gave my name a certain tragic dimension and a whole new feel when it was pronounced in French. But I wondered if my uncle had read the book before he wrapped it up and gave it to me? Before he wrote "For our own Miss Julie" on the banknote?

Are my grandfather's boots in any way associated with the count's boots? Did Miss Julie come? It's impossible to say. Did Anna Karenina come? The same Anna Karenina who sacrificed everything for love? Dear God, let's hope she came.

Writing about *Miss Julie* is obviously not going to work, but completing the diary of Eva Braun is a brilliant idea. This is what I've been waiting for; the book has to be written.

I HAVEN'T MASTURBATED yet today, and it's almost noon. The rest of the family might need me at any moment.

THE PHONE RINGS. It's Cecilie. We grew up together. She's an architect and, like most female architects, Cecilie has a husband who is also an architect. They seem to get along and have shared interests — they walk in the countryside and do all that. They are irritatingly successful and happy. That's what I usually think whenever I meet her, which is fortunately not very often. For as long as I can remember, we have competed with each other in some way. We so desperately want to show the other that we're doing well, that our choices in life have been right.

"So, are you writing anything at the moment?" Cecilie asks.

I could have told her about my orgasm project, but decide not to. Cecilie is of course someone who comes — someone who has the correct, relaxed attitude to her sexuality. I feel the urge to tell Cecilie to go to hell.

Instead, I tell her about my Eva Braun project with exuberant enthusiasm. I've done quite a lot on it already, I tell her. For the first time in ages I'm enjoying my work, I say. Cecilie is quiet.

"Don't you think it will be good?"

Cecilie says nothing.

"Well? Don't you think it will be good?" I ask again.

"I mean, it's a great idea, but hasn't it been done before?"

"Oh."

"I think it was called *The Devil's Mistress*. Came out in the nineties."

"Was it any good?" I try to keep my composure.

"Um, yes, I think so. It's been so long since I read it. Actually, yes, now that I think about it, *The Devil's Mistress* was in fact very good."

Of course. Of course someone else has written a *very good* continuation of Eva Braun's diary.

"Are you there?"

"Yes, where else would I be?"

Is Cecilie gloating? Does she get a sense of satisfaction from this? It's not easy to tell.

"Ah well, I better get something done today," she

says abruptly, as though she is far busier than me, with a thousand projects waiting.

"I've got an au pair," I say.

"And does it help? I mean, isn't that a bit much when you work from home?"

"I got her so I could make time to masturbate." The words just pop out of my mouth.

Cecilie is dumbstruck. It's wonderful. Normally she has too much to say. She could just think that I'm being immature, so immature that she can't be bothered to answer.

Perhaps her silence is more resigned exasperation.

After what feels like a lifetime, Cecilie says again that it's time to get things done.

"Absolutely," I say, and feel that, in a way, I've won.

I can't be bothered to masturbate, and I can't write.

I can hear Ludmila boiling the kettle in the kitchen. It builds up to a kind of crescendo that has never bothered me before, but recently it's started to drive me mad. She normally brews something slimy and green, which I guess is seaweed, but I've never wanted to investigate. Some sort of Ukrainian sludge, that's for sure. I decide to postpone my masturbation project until tomorrow. I just don't feel like it today. I get out of bed, take a deep breath and go up into the kitchen. Because of the situation, I'm still in my bathrobe. Ludmila looks at me with some skepticism.

"Are you not going to work?"

"I don't go to work, Ludmila. And in any case, it's Saturday."

There's a flicker of uncertainty in her eyes.

"You write books?"

"Yes, sometimes."

"But not today?"

"No, not today. Not on a Saturday."

I notice that the sink is full of green gunk.

"I'll tidy up," she says swiftly.

"Good," I say.

The doorbell rings. I point to my attire, indicating that Ludmila has to answer. She's already on her way.

"It's for me," she calls, and I catch a glimpse of Michael in the hallway and retreat quietly back downstairs.

I suddenly remember the sofa coverings that are lying in a black garbage bag in the bathroom, and decide to go to the dry cleaners. It will do me some good to get out. A thinks it's a good idea. The children want to come with me, but I say no.

"What's up with you?" A asks.

"I just need some time to myself, is that so strange?"

"Yes, considering that you're alone most of the day, it is," A replies.

THE MAN AT the dry cleaners is different from the men I know. I know lots of different types of men, but none like him. He has big hands and rough, tanned skin. He's how I imagine a craftsman should be, but I'm not sure that you can call a dry cleaner a craftsman. I think his wife actually runs the business. She's old and ugly. He's just old and dangerous. If the dry cleaning man asked to sleep with me, I would do it. And I would have an orgasm. Guaranteed. But I wouldn't fall in love with the dry cleaning man. Or would I?

THE DRY CLEANING man reminds me of Harvey Keitel in the *The Piano*. Then I think that perhaps I should be thinking of *Miss Julie*. Could the dry cleaning man be Jean? No. The dry cleaning man exudes contentment. He definitely doesn't know any French words. He's happy with life in his clogs, rolling around like a happy seal between the counter and the rail of coat hangers and strangers' coats. He has no wish to be upwardly mobile. I have no doubt. Maybe that's what makes him attractive—that he seems to be so totally content?

I brush the hair away from my face and smile as provocatively as I can. I try to make my lips fuller and my eyes narrower, but it doesn't work. For a moment, I've forgotten that I'm here to clean a sofa cover that's smeared with shit.

I quickly tighten my lips and hand the humiliating garbage bag over the counter.

"It's a sofa cover," I say, looking down.

"What have you got on it?"

"Poo," I say, blushing.

Poo is, of course, an ordinary word in my world; I use it several times a day. I talk to other mothers and fathers almost daily who also see the word as perfectly normal, but here in the dry cleaners it has suddenly becomes an embarrassing word to use. The dry cleaning man has long since forgotten poo. His children, if he has any, have long since grown up. They don't "poo" anymore.

"Shit," I say, hastily, as if that were more grown up.

He raises his eyebrows.

"Oops."

I feel the need to explain that I'm the mother of two small children who are no better or worse than any other children, two small children who poo on the sofa while watching Mickey Mouse Clubhouse, but instead I say, "But it's not my shit."

The dry cleaning man doesn't seem that interested.

"We'll see what we can do. And just so you know, it's not always easy to get covers like this back on after they've been cleaned."

He could at least have pretended to be interested. I sulk.

"There we go," he says, and hands me a receipt. I nod and take it.

"Mommy! Mommy! Where are you? What are you doing?"

Mr. Rabbit is up on his hind legs inside me. I'm thinking about the dry cleaning man and his big, coarse hands stroking me. He calls me *little one* and talks dirty to me.

"I'm in the bedroom. I'll be coming soon."

Liva is back and will be going out again to her gymnastics class soon. I've forgotten to pack her kit.

"Where are my plimsolls?"

"They're on the shelf in the laundry room."

"What are we having for dinner?"

"We can talk about that later. Go and get your plimsolls first."

"What's that noise?"

"Go and get your shoes."

There's silence outside the door. Then I hear: "Mom. Are you coming? I'm going over to Andrea's before gymnastics."

"Yes, I'm coming in a minute," I respond, and can't help thinking how ridiculous this everyday sentence has become.

L IVA EXERCISES, BUT it's me who should be exercising. Perhaps something might happen if I did more exercise? *Dagbladet* certainly seems to think so. Atle Jansen writes about an important scientific study that actually *proves* that exercise can give women an orgasm:

> *The findings of a new study carried out by Indiana University in the United States confirm that women can have a "coregasm," an orgasm triggered by training the core muscles in the abdominal region. It is usually abdominal exercises, such as pole dancing, cycling, spinning, and weightlifting that result in orgasm.*

The scientist interviewed about the study has no explanation as to what actually happens in these women's bodies, but she finds the data interesting since it indicates that orgasms are not necessarily a sexual event, which might help us to understand more about the underlying processes in a woman's body when she's having an orgasm.

The people working on the study have not yet identified the proportion of women who have had "coregasms" while training, but it only took five weeks to recruit for further study 370 women who allege that they have experienced coregasms. The scientists would therefore not say that it was an uncommon phenomenon.

So they're telling me it's normal, and I can't do it. I have an exercise bike, and I use it often, but I have never been close to having an orgasm while using it. Quite the opposite: I've waited for the clock on the digital screen to show me when enough minutes have passed that it's legitimate to get off and do something more productive. I don't like exercise; perhaps that's where the problem lies. You have to learn to enjoy it, the feeling of endorphins flooding your body; that way, you're not hindered by things like a cold or the fact that you're tired. When I exercise, I long to get off the bike, but not only that, I long to get away from my body, from its deficiencies. And there are more of them than ever: the stiffness in my hips, my knee that seizes up, the lack of flexibility in my neck. This is a body that doesn't come when I'm exercising, a body that doesn't have coregasms. A body that refuses to do what the scientists say is not an uncommon phenomenon. I'll try to give the exercise bike another chance. It stands beside the bed, reminding me of all that I should have done. I should cycle for at least an hour a day. I promised A I would use it that often when I found it online and he drove well beyond the city boundaries to pick it up.

"It'll just end up gathering dust," he said.

"No, I'm really motivated this time," I assured him.

He set off reluctantly, and for the first few weeks I felt obliged to use the bike. I forced myself to do half an hour every evening. But never, not even for one second, has it given me any form of erotic satisfaction. Now the bike functions perfectly as a drying rack. It's practical for both fitted sheets and socks. Whenever A remarks that it's gathering dust, I point this out to him.

"Wouldn't it have been cheaper to buy a clothesline?"

"I'm sure it would," I say.

But now I'm ready for a coregasm. I get onto the saddle naked and pedal furiously as I try to visualize Don Draper from *Mad Men* (despite the fact that lots of women don't even need to *think* about sex to get an orgasm while training). And do I feel anything?

Yes. There's a stirring. Don and I are on a date. He's even better looking and more mysterious than on TV, but the smoking annoys me. *Do you have to puff on that all the time?* And I certainly can't live with his views on women. *Who do you think you are?* Dark and mysterious, but useless as a husband and father.

And who am I, anyway? Do I really want to ruin his marriage? To disappoint a beautiful young wife who now finally, in season six, has made a breakthrough in her acting career? No, I'm actually not interested in the chain-smoking idiot. I get off the bike and lie down on the bed.

I want to call a sexologist to ask what he or she thinks my problem is, but I don't dare. I'm simply too shy. Perhaps I shouldn't be. "Sexologist" is not a protected title. Anyone can claim to be a sexologist. I could call myself one if I wanted to. And when the week is over, perhaps I should. Who knows?

Maybe I could call Atle Jansen instead? He's obviously in the know when it comes to female sexuality. I google his name. He turns out to be a slightly overweight man in his prime. The photographs on the Internet are anything but threatening. The fact that he's a little portly is without a doubt endearing. He's also good at skiing. I watch a short video that seems to suggest that he beat Anette Bøe in a sprint at Holmenkollen in 2011. I don't manage to find out whether he's married, but he looks as though he is. And last but not least: he won the SKUP Award in 2007 for something he wrote about oil workers in the North Sea. His journalistic expertise is wide ranging, that's for sure. How does Atle Jansen decide to write about the things he does? What drives him?

I hear A and the children clattering in upstairs. Liva has clearly come back from gymnastics, too. I put on some sweatpants and go up into the living room. Ludmila and Martin are there. Dinner is ready: burnt sausages with some kind of Ukrainian sauce.

"What have you been up to?" A asks.

"Nothing in particular." I reply.

"Running? Cycling?"

"Absolutely not," I say, and go back down to the bedroom.

WHEN I'M BACK in bed, I call Vibeke and tell her that I can't go see a movie. She's annoyed.

"You always cancel at the last minute."

"Not always," I say, and hang up.

Vibeke is a lesbian. She's the happiest friend I've got. She had a long-term relationship with her teacher from high school, but they broke up a couple of years ago. I think she has a very open and easy attitude to her sexuality. And then it hits me—it's Vibeke I should be talking to. She must know all about the vagina and female orgasms. I call her again and ask if we can meet after the film.

"Alone," I say.

"How exciting," Vibeke teases.

"Don't tell the others that you're going to meet me," I ask.

"Okay," Vibeke replies.

I haven't been with a woman before, not like that. But there was an episode in Israel, something that I remember as surprising—that felt like something more.

THE ROOF OF the casino is flat, and from up there you can see the sunset and the fishing boat lights. Norman from South Africa has moved in. He's been in Israel a long time. The South Africa he left no longer exists. The home he once had has new rules and new laws, so he thinks he'll just stay here. A young Israeli girl named Tamara, who has escaped from a kibbutz in the north, shows up after Norman. He's brought her to the casino. She had an argument with her parents and wants to learn to stand on her own two feet. She certainly doesn't want to go back to the kibbutz. She's eighteen years old and very angry. We let her stay. And when she brings her English girlfriend, Melanie, who's in her twenties, from Bristol, we let her stay, too. Why not? There's space.

There were other people at the casino at the time, people who came and went, but I've forgotten their names and faces. I haven't forgotten Tamara; I remember

Tamara. Her black eyes, curly hair, and the vein on her neck that used to pulse in a way that initially made me think of life, and then later death.

It's early May, and we've got a battery-powered radio on the roulette table. We hear on the news that a bomb has exploded on a bus somewhere in the north. Lots of people have been killed — ten or fifteen. It will take some time to put the bodies together, like a jigsaw puzzle of hands and heads. It's very hot outside, the kind of warm, heavy air you can hold in your hands. Tamara, Melanie, and I are sitting at the table drinking water. Tamara translates what's being said on the radio. She seems to be upset.

"I'm ashamed of being an Israeli," she says, as though she realizes what we're thinking and feels the need to defend herself.

We don't say anything. She's only eighteen.

We play cards. It's still too hot to go outside. Tamara is supposed to go to her job in a fish restaurant, but she can't be bothered. There are lots of jobs, and you can always find a new one if you've got enough money to tide you over.

There's a news update on the radio every hour. By the time the names of the dead are read out at six p.m., Tamara and Melanie are on ecstasy. I'm not quite sure whether Tamara is laughing or crying when they read out her mother's name. Jesus, I didn't even know it was her mother's name, but the name triggers a response. She buries her head in her thin, brown arms. Her shoulders shake. It sounds like she's laughing, but it's a disturbing laughter that sounds more like crying.

She jerks her head back, as though someone has just woken her, but she still says nothing. I notice that the vein on her neck is throbbing more violently than usual. It could be the heat or the E capsule. She gets into the shower with her clothes on and then drags herself dripping onto the roof. Melanie sits up there with her. I turn on the TV and see images of the bombed-out bus.

"Come with me?" she asks sometime later.

Her voice is so quiet; she suddenly seems so little, standing there with her black, bottomless eyes. I've already slept for a few hours and the Englishman is lying beside me. It must be somewhere between midnight and one.

She's going to the kibbutz because her father wants her there, and she wants to be there, too, she says. I slip out of the Englishman's arms, pull a cotton dress over my head, and follow Tamara out.

It's almost a three-hour taxi ride. Her hand rests in my lap and slides under my dress and in between my legs. Her fingers move rhythmically. I don't say anything and try to work out if the driver can see what's happening in the rear-view mirror. Neither of us have money to pay for the taxi.

"I've been so incredibly naive," she says, out of the blue.

She talks without drawing her hand away, and it continues to move rhythmically between my legs, as though it were disconnected from the rest of her body. I want her to keep going.

"What?" I gasp.

"I left the kibbutz because it wasn't liberal enough, because they wouldn't give the Palestinians more land, because they wouldn't treat them the same way they treat Israelis. And what happens? They were right all along! I should have listened to them. Mom always said that we had to protect what was ours, and I was always adamant that it wasn't ours — that we'd stolen the land — but Mom didn't steal anything, she lived and worked on the kibbutz just like her mother and grandmother did. She didn't steal anything!"

I look out at the desert they're fighting about. I'm not going to come now either.

The sun is starting to rise when we arrive at the kibbutz. A Doberman comes bounding towards us and seems to know Tamara. It licks my juices from her hand. Lights go on in the houses, and a man who must be her father comes out and pays for the taxi without saying anything. He's a small, thin man. I wonder if he had been bigger before tonight.

DID I COME in the taxi? Maybe I need a woman, or maybe the idea of death helps. Death crops up everywhere, as if death and sex are inextricably linked. I ponder this before going out to meet Vibeke.

VIBEKE STARES AT me over the table.

"Never? You've *never* had an orgasm?"

I shake my head.

"Is that possible?"

"Obviously it is," I say, smarting, with a shrug.

"But then you need help."

She is clearly upset about the whole thing and tosses her head back, sending her dark curls dancing. Her voice cuts through the background noise of the café. People look at us and no doubt wonder what I need help with.

"Shh! I'm trying to help myself," I say.

"And how's that going?"

I shake my head and tell her about Mr. Rabbit and Condomania's orgasm guarantee. "It's not going at all."

"Oh, you poor thing. Have some wine," Vibeke says, pouring me a glass. "You should have come to me before," she continues. "If there's anyone who knows how women work, it's me. Don't worry, we'll fix it."

Why didn't I think of Vibeke before? Isn't she the most obvious solution? I know I'm not a lesbian, but that doesn't mean that my clitoris can't be stimulated by someone who is — someone who knows about these things.

Suddenly I feel well cared for and engulfed in the wine. I think I should drink more often. Vibeke definitely seems to know what she's talking about.

"Do you have to go home tonight?" she asks, putting her hand on my shoulder.

"No, I've got an au pair," I reply.

"Of course you have an au pair."

There is nothing I won't try, I decide. I go out and call A to say that I'm going to stay over at Vibeke's.

"It's been a hard week," I say.

"Has it?" he asks with disbelief.

"Without a doubt," I say.

Suddenly Vibeke is behind me with her hand on my shoulder.

"The bill's sorted," she says.

VIBEKE KISSES ME and it's not like kissing a man; it feels softer. In an odd way, the fact that I shouldn't be doing this — or feel that I shouldn't be doing this — turns me on. I allow myself to get carried away and let my hands glide down over her bony, thin, curving back, a narrow womanly shape that feels unfamiliar.

The wine sings in my head. I feel dizzy, like I bumped my head on something.

Vibeke strokes my back as we kiss. Not gingerly, in the way I stroke her, but with intent. I'm confused. Vibeke continues to caress me as her hand slowly moves further down my body. She tells me to lie on the bed, and sits behind me. I'm still lying on my stomach. I don't understand what she's doing, but my mind is like a cotton ball. I'll do anything and am hardly aware of it when she takes hold of my hips and wants me to lift up my ass. She guides me with determined hands. I let myself be lifted with a strength I had no idea she possessed in that slight frame of hers. Seconds later, three fingers glide into me with no resistance because I'm so wet. She moves her fingers in and out several times. I can feel her thumb on my clitoris, massaging the soft folds of skin around the opening while her fingers move inside, gently pressing against the walls of my vagina. I feel myself building to a climax. Something is actually going to happen this time! Vibeke was right when she said she knew all about women; she knows what she's doing.

Then suddenly it all just comes gushing out. I give a muted sob.

"You should have said you were feeling sick," Vibeke says with indignation.

"I didn't know it was happening," I mumble apologetically, as I try to avoid drowning in my own vomit.

"Those are Susanne Schjerning pillows," she points out.

"I know. I'm sorry. I'll have them dry cleaned for you," I say, thinking that it's another opportunity to see the dry cleaning man.

"Probably best if we get some sleep," Vibeke sighs, leaving me uncertain as to whether she's accepted my offer or not.

DAY 5

THERE'S HARDLY A soul to be seen. It's half past five and I'm trying not to think about yesterday. I should never drink.

Vibeke gave me a very thorough introduction to the vagina's potential.

She gave it her best. She did everything she knows is right. And I liked it.

But it didn't work. When I close my eyes and think of her fingers inside me, I just feel embarrassed.

The orgasm guarantee is about to run out. I've got only three days left, and I still haven't come. And then there's Eva Braun; she keeps invading my thoughts. It's distracting. First I was excited about coming up with a new book topic. Now I'm preoccupied with the disappointment of discovering that someone else has had the idea before me.

I try not to think about it. I'm generally just too wound up. I don't feel free enough. Maybe I should just forget the whole Eva Braun project. Maybe it's actually a blessing that someone else has done it before. It dawns on me that I should, of course, write some erotica instead. Maybe that would help to open me up? But can I write erotica? It wouldn't be the first time. I tried to write an erotic short story when I was twenty-one. I took a break from my studies to earn some money, and moved back home with my parents. The first job I had was to look after an old lady in a nursing home named Margit. She had an enormous hernia. It hung out of her stomach, a bulge of fat and flesh. It would kill her in the end and she knew it.

"Everyone dies of something," she said.

I washed and cleaned the hernia every day. Her breasts were heavy, and I had to lift them up with one hand, and wash underneath with the other. I also had to tend to her bedsores, which sometimes got infected; the doctor, who came once a week, had to give her a prescription for antibiotics.

The first time I was there, I gagged and had to rush to the toilet. I had to lie to Margit and say that I had a tummy bug.

Then it got easier. After a week, I lifted her breasts as if it was the most natural thing in the world, cleaned her hernia, and washed her crotch. I embraced her body with a kind of routine love.

I read crime fiction and that sort of thing to her,

which she liked. But then one day I got there and she put a book in my lap and said, "Read that!"

It was Anaïs Nin's *Delta of Venus*. I started to laugh. Margit looked offended.

"You think it just fizzles out?" she asked.

"Of course not," I replied, but the truth was that I did. I thought it just fizzled out.

And so I read. I read about golden brown penises that were polished like bats, about tongues, and about intestines and sexual orifices.

I couldn't look at Margit while I read. I kept my eyes firmly on the page, my cheeks burning. I think I got as far as page sixty-seven before I glanced over at her and discovered that she had died. She looked very peaceful.

The next day, weighed down by the knowledge that life is short, I decided to find a lover. I fell for a lodger who was living at my parents' house at the time. He worked in the oil industry and had a wife and children in Oslo, whom he went home to every weekend. He was a polite and mature man. We had only met briefly in the driveway a few times, and chatted about the wind and weather. I asked whether he was happy in the apartment and town in general. Mom told me about his wife and children. I thought it was an advantage. I didn't want a boyfriend; I wanted a man with some experience who would teach me what I didn't know about sex. I would never have done anything like that now, and I can't believe that I even dared. In our brief encounters out in the driveway, he had never given me any signs that he was interested in me, not even a flirty look. There was nothing to indicate that he was anything other than a happy family man who was doing what he had to do to look after his wife and children. But on the day after Margit died, I went down to his apartment and knocked on the door. It was raining lightly and I had nothing on under Dad's old raincoat. I had watched the nurses prepare Margit's body. They had washed her hernia and breasts, wiped away the excrement, dressed her in white, and folded her hands over her chest. I'd sat by the bed and read the rest of *Delta of Venus*.

It's possible that I drew my courage from that experience. The raincoat was cold and I could feel my nipples hardening against the waxed fabric. The lodger didn't look surprised when he opened the door.

"Oh, it's you," he said, as if he knew me, like I was someone who popped by all the time.

He opened the door and invited me in. I waited for him to ask what I wanted, and thought hard about what I would say when he did. The circumstances were titillating; here I was trying to bed a lodger living in my childhood home—well, almost my childhood home. The studio apartment was the only part of the house where we children were not allowed to go, because it was always either rented out or locked. In the summer, it was used by visiting relatives from Oslo. We would run down in the morning to wake cousins and aunts, but we were always there as guests. It didn't feel like home, even though I could see our old china in the cabinet in the tiny living room.

"Would you like a cup of tea?" he asked.

I could hear Mom's footsteps overhead and all the other sounds of the house, only they felt the wrong way around down here. She was taking things out of the dishwasher and I could hear the glasses, cutlery, and plates finding their respective homes.

"I just want you," I said, opening my coat as if it were theatre curtains at the start of a performance. He stepped back. Then I dropped the coat to the ground. He stared at my body for a few short seconds before he turned away.

"The news," he said. "The news is about to begin. I always watch it. Sorry."

He closed the door to the living room, and I was left standing in the entrance, naked, with my dad's raincoat around my ankles. Mom dropped something on the floor upstairs and I heard her calling my name.

Some months later *Cupido* magazine ran a short story competition, and a friend of my mine encouraged me to give it a try. I wrote something about going to visit my parents' lodger and described how he greeted me and then impaled me on his great spear and yearned for

IT'S NEARLY TEN in the morning when I get home. Martin is asleep. The little ones are outside playing, Liva is in her room, and Ludmila is nowhere to be seen.

"What did you and Vibeke get up to yesterday?" A asks.

"Nothing in particular," I reply, walking over to the fridge. I open it so that I can hide behind the door.

"You're acting weird," A states.

Have I been unfaithful? Physically, yes, there's no doubt, but emotionally I'm not so sure. And I'm fairly certain that if I told A what had happened he would find it exciting. He would definitely just laugh about the spew.

"Not at all," I say, and pop my head around the fridge door with a smile that's as relaxed as possible.

"Do you want something to eat?"

"No thanks," I reply.

"So why are you looking in the fridge then?"

"Don't know. Think I might go and lie down for a bit."

A shrugs, but I can tell that he's annoyed.

I fall asleep as soon as I lie down, and when I wake up it's almost evening.

DAY 6

A AND THE kids have left. It's the start of a new week and the world outside carries on as usual. I would love to be a part of that routine machinery, part of what works. I put my feet down onto the floor, thrust up my pelvis, and let the vibrator loose. It's fantastic. I'm actually enjoying it, and think that perhaps my time with Vibeke was fruitful and that it's opened me up in some way, despite all the embarrassment. I'm still a bit tired from the weekend and close my eyes and let out a soft moan. The moaning is confirmation that what I'm doing is actually turning me on. Suddenly I hear a thump. Something bangs against the window. I put down Mr. Rabbit and grab my bathrobe. I draw the curtains and look out into the garden. There's a great tit lying on the ground. I put on my slippers and go out onto the frozen lawn. The bird is lying on its side. When I bend down and lift it up, it's still warm. I assume that it's dead, even though its body is still throbbing, like an echo of its pulse. I close my hands around the bird's body and think that I'll put it in a box, so that the children can help me bury it when they get home. Then suddenly it flies away, as though my hands have given it life again.

LUDMILA IS BUSY up in the kitchen. She's promised A to make cabbage rolls, since they are apparently his favourite dish. I had no idea that A liked cabbage rolls before Ludmila came here. I'm dreading dinner already. I get dressed and go up to the kitchen to get Martin. He's happy to see me, and I take him back down with me, but he doesn't want to be cuddled on the bed. He wants to be near the action and crawls back up the stairs to Ludmila, who lets him empty the kitchen drawers. The parquet will be covered in scratches.

I lie on the bed and do nothing. My vagina is sting-ing. Soon I hear the rest of the family coming home, kicking off their shoes, and throwing their jackets on the floor. Ludmila tells everyone that the cabbage rolls are ready.

"**D**ELICIOUS," A EXCLAIMS enthusiastically.

I push the cabbage rolls around my plate. I don't want them to be good, but they are—ridiculously good.

"Do you not like them, Julie?"

A sends me a questioning look. Ludmila is lording it up at the head of the table. She's got red splotches on her neck and looks proud and happy. Her triumphant face is enough to put me off my food.

"Yes, but they're a bit dry, perhaps?"

"Here, have some sauce," Ludmila says immediately.

I thank her and pour some sauce over my diner. It tastes delicious, but I can feel that it must be full of fat.

"Yes, they're dangerously good, but we can't have it again otherwise we'll be as fat as pigs in no time."

"I don't want to be fat as a pig," Liva wails.

"And you won't be, darling," A says, calming her down and sending me a dirty look.

"Have you had enough?"

A nods and Ludmila gets up and starts to clear the table, her movements quick and efficient; she's buoyed by all the praise.

I hear Alva asking for another helping. She hasn't asked for seconds since I made meat soup for Michael and his men.

I T WAS THE week before Michael and his men were
due to build the sleeping platform. Martin was
burbling away happily in the stroller. It hadn't rained
for weeks. The sky was almost alarmingly blue and the
air was cold and sharp. I walked and walked, loving
every minute of it. The tingling air on my cheeks and
in my lungs felt so good. When we got back from our
walk, Michael and his friends were standing outside
the neighbour's house smoking. They had been working
since seven in the morning and would continue working until ten at night. I felt sorry for them. For some
reason or other, I wanted to do something that would
make them happy. Surely they would want some food,
I thought. Heating up a can of soup requires no effort
and it might be good for them to have something warm.
I decided to pop down to the supermarket to do some
shopping. Martin had fallen asleep straightaway and
would be sleeping now for another couple of hours,

so I had time to make proper soup from scratch. If I invited the neighbours or some friends over, I would never serve them canned soup, so why shouldn't the Poles have homemade soup, too? Didn't they need it more than anyone else?

I bought some beef, vegetables, flat-leaf parsley, and chives, and gave the workers a little wink when I went by with my bags.

Martin woke up just before I finished chopping the vegetables. He had only been asleep for half an hour. I tried to rock him back to sleep, but it didn't work. The onion that I was browning got burnt, and I had to pick Martin up and chop another one. Martin was grouchy and wanted milk, but I chopped the onion with tears in my eyes and then sat down with him and cried.

The soup wasn't ready until well after lunchtime. On the other hand, I had nearly ten litres, so there was enough for us to have it for supper. I set the table out on the deck and put out some bowls and flatbread before going over to inform the men that lunch was ready.

I felt a rush of anticipation about telling the oblivious workers that I would be serving them lunch on the terrace. They would be completely surprised, and I imagined Michael's amber eyes lighting up with gratitude.

It felt good to be doing something for others, but as I got closer, I suddenly felt unsure. By the time I was standing in front of them, I had no idea what to say. Michael spotted me and Martin, who was sitting in my arms chewing on a biscuit. He came over, smiling.

"Sunday?"

I nodded.

Michael turned to leave.

"I, uh...made some lunch," I stammered.

"Ah," Michael said.

Unfortunately, I didn't know what "ah" meant.

"Do you want some?"

"No, no," he said casually. "We've already eaten. We need to work."

And before I could say any more, Michael had climbed up a ladder. He said something to one of the men who was carrying a bag of cement. The man looked over at me and laughed. I held Martin tighter and pressed my nose into his sweater. I felt so incredibly foolish.

My first thought was that A must never know. If he came home and saw ten litres of meat soup on the stove, he would want an explanation; if I told him the truth, he would accuse me of being egotistical and self-centred.

A would use it against me. He would say that I only think of myself and ask me why I hadn't run it by the workers first. "Why do you assume that everyone else has the same needs as you?" he would ask.

And I *had* forgotten to ask them if they wanted the

soup, but who wouldn't want warm soup? Surely every-one wants that.

I emptied about half the soup down the toilet, leaving enough for a decent supper.

A studied the soup in his spoon, and then rolled it around his mouth as though he was tasting wine.

"Good soup," he said.

"Thank you," I replied.

"Made from scratch?"

I nodded.

"I want more," Alva piped up.

"You like it as well? Mommy made it herself," A said.

"There isn't any more," I said. I hadn't expected them to eat so much. Alva slipped down from her chair. Martin was already playing on the floor.

"You'll have to make more next time," A smiled.

"Yes," I said. "Next time I'll make more."

ALVA GETS ANOTHER helping of cabbage rolls. I obviously don't like them as much as the rest of the family. I take Martin with me down to the TV room, so I don't have to watch Ludmila stacking the dishwasher.

"Does it bother you that she makes such good food?" A follows me down the stairs.

"What do you mean?"

"You know perfectly well what I mean."

"I have no idea what you're talking about," I say, giving A a warning look.

He slowly grins, as if to say *you know exactly what I mean.* I leave Martin with A and go into the bedroom and lock the door. I find another article by Atle Jansen about coregasms on the Internet. He refers to the article he wrote a couple of days prior about getting coregasms from exercising. Now he says that you don't even need to exercise to have an orgasm—you can simply breathe.

He profiles a Swedish woman named Mita, an "erotic consultant," who can achieve orgasm using some simple breathing exercises, without any accessories.

Atle explains that all she does is tighten her pelvic floor muscles so that they connect with the clitoris. When she feels contact, she clenches and breathes, and keeps breathing until she comes.

I click on the embedded link that opens a video of Mita in action. The TV reporter doing the interview looks a bit embarrassed, but Mita doesn't seem to mind the attention at all and just carries on breathing her way to orgasm.

"Oh god, that was great," she says, when she's finished demonstrating the technique.

My first thought when I see Mita lying in the bridge position, breathing, is that I could fake that. Perhaps Mita is faking, too? She is breathing heavily in and out, with her eyes shut. She arches her pelvis forward as she strokes her stomach. She is a person without shame; she is totally free. I can't help thinking she's ridiculous, but I wonder if that's just the envy talking. Am I jealous of Mita the sex consultant from Sweden because she is shameless?

I tried to be shameless the time I let Dad's raincoat slip off my shoulders in the entrance to my parents' lodger's apartment, but it didn't work. So I took the virtuous path instead. I went back to dating athletes. My new boyfriend played football in the top league; that's to say, the third division in my hometown. The players commanded enormous local respect. Businesses would do whatever they could for the players: team members got car stereos and food processors, and free tickets. They also got women. My football player was not a handsome man, but he oozed confidence, which I thought was sexy. When we met at the local pub, his team had just lost for the third time in a row, but he didn't seem too bothered about it.

I promptly told him that I hated football and would never sleep with him. Since he was a competitive person, this marked the official start of what I would later think of as "the hunt." I doubt he was ever in love with me, but it was not in his nature to lose — certainly not off the football pitch. The next morning, he had ten red roses delivered to my door. Mom said they were the most expensive kind of flowers, so I gave them to her. When he called later that day, I explained that she loved them. I knew that I would sleep with him eventually, but I also knew that once we'd had sex, he would dump me and find someone new to pursue. It was possibly a form of prostitution, but I decided to get as much as possible out of the situation. We went for expensive meals. He bought me a Walkman. I got tickets to all the matches, but I never used them, much to his annoyance.

He took me out for dinner with his teammates. They all had girlfriends who were slim, blonde, and very young mothers. It was obvious that he was slightly ashamed of me, and thought I said stupid things.

I felt awkward but also utterly superior to these other women, who I thought would never get any further in life. They had already found their places in the world and would do nothing other than age. I couldn't understand why they hadn't chosen to study and travel, as I had.

When we did eventually have sex, it was not what I had expected at all. I made him wait three months. His team was in danger of being relegated to the fourth division, which I had understood to be a catastrophe, and he was generally in a bad mood. I had become accustomed to having him around, to feeling his hands around my waist, between my legs, and in my hair. I couldn't back out now: rules were rules. So I rose to the occasion and the sex was unexpectedly good. He had a beautiful body, like the men in Anaïs Nin's short stories. He didn't throw himself at me, as I might have guessed he would after such a long courtship. On the contrary: he took his time and I breathed in the smell of this body that I had got so used to having near me. He had slept with lots of women and did things that I didn't know were possible.

I wasn't his type. We had nothing of any significance to talk about, but the relationship staggered on. The football season was coming to an end. Then he dumped me and I wept bitter tears, which I had never imagined I would. I went to a football match for the first time; it was the last of the year. It was raining and I shouted his name in the downpour along with the other fans in the stands.

"Come on," I shouted. "Come back to me," I yelled, everyone around me oblivious to the words I'd really said.

It was clear that the team was going to be relegated by the end of the match, and I wasn't the only one crying when I left the stadium.

I'm quite sure that he would have made me have an orgasm if he had just been a bit more patient.

WHEN I MET A, the daily drudge began. I obviously wasn't aware of it back then because it sails under a false flag, and you don't recognize it until you're there.

I MET HIM in a bar. I'd just written my first novel, which was being published by one of the country's big publishing houses, a fact that might explain his initial interest in me. It wasn't an easy start. A had been dumped that spring by his girlfriend of two years. It was autumn and he was still on the rebound. He said that he wasn't able to feel anything and that he wasn't in love with me.

"Yes, you are," I said.

"No, I'm not," he said.

"Yes, you're in love," I pressed, and after two months he admitted that it might be true; he was *possibly* in love. Things moved fast from there. He stayed over at my place more and more often and moved in after a few months. Our hearts fizzed over. I was ecstatically happy and didn't keep in touch with my friends. I was in love with someone for the first time and there was nothing anyone could do to stop me from caring for him. I looked for flaws, tried to find weaknesses or any dependencies he might have, but found nothing.

My apartment was too small for him. It had low ceilings, and the rooms shrank when he walked through them. The furniture that he insisted on moving in with him didn't fit, but none of that mattered because I felt so secure. Everything felt right, and I was thinking about the future. I thought we could happily have children; something that had been previously unthinkable was suddenly a possible future, almost a wish. I flirted with the idea that a new life could grow in me.

We stayed up at night, ate spaghetti, and listened to Cornelis Vreeswijk. We had stopped being anyone other than ourselves, and it still worked. I faked an orgasm the first time we had sex. I'd had lots of practice by that point, and A was obviously impressed, but for the first time it felt wrong to fake it.

We were terribly in love. He was everything I had ever dreamed of and, more importantly, he was completely normal. He didn't drink or beat me. He would definitely get a good job when he completed his qualifications. I wanted to have his children, and I faked some

I WAS ON a boat when I discovered I was pregnant. Everything was heaving and I felt sick. The father of my child was watching a football match with some boys who were about sixteen. A was making loud, opinionated comments about the match, as if he was in his own living room. I could tell that the boys thought my boyfriend was annoying—and old. I didn't feel old; I certainly didn't feel old enough to have a child.

I was going to do a master's degree. I was going to write several novels. I was going to travel. *Then* I was going to have children. But only once I'd finished another degree, travelled, and written my books. That was the plan.

THE STORM WAS not over. The boat rocked and I continued to heave. For several days I hadn't eaten anything other than Danish chicken salad, which I then threw up. The whole experience felt like something out of *The Perfect Storm*. There really was a lot of wind.

It wasn't easy to take a pregnancy test in a storm, but I managed in the end. I put the stick down on the moving sink. It was supposed to lie flat and horizontal for a minute, but horizontal didn't exist in this weather. The boat was moving and rocking all the time, shaking the test and shaking me and the child that might be inside me. I sat with my eyes closed for minute and waited for the answer: two blue lines.

Would I be able to look after a child? Would it be a boy or a girl? Would it be more like me or the boy sitting outside? I lay on the floor of Deck 3 that night and held on to an artificial palm tree while the storm raged. Fortunately the palm tree was chained to the wall like the child, or fetus, was chained to me, tied down with a cord of blood and food.

The child's father was playing bingo with an old lady. He had red felt pen on his forehead. His face lit up when he saw me.

"Hi," he said.

"I'm pregnant," I told him.

"That's fantastic news," he replied and carried on playing bingo.

"I'm pregnant," I repeated.

"Relax, we've got nine months to plan everything," he said.

"Eight," I retorted.

"There's certainly no rush," he said.

The storm died down over the course of the afternoon. Someone announced there would be free food in all the restaurants on the top deck because the canteen had been smashed to pieces during the night.

I was the first to arrive and was starving, having spent the entire night throwing up. I won the race to the head waiter. He was wearing white gloves and some kind of uniform.

I suddenly didn't feel very presentable and regretted not brushing my teeth. He asked how many people we would be.

"One...and a half," I said, desperately trying to tidy up my braids.

"So, a table for one," the head waiter confirmed.

"Yes," I agreed. I was shown to a table at the very back of the room. The buffet looked amazing, with pork and sauerkraut, salmon and sausages. I piled up my plate.

In the middle of mouthful number five, I felt like I was going to be sick. I looked around for the nearest toilet, but could only see the other passengers pouring in from all quarters, focused on the free food; old women who had torn themselves away from the slots, drunk football supporters, and families with small children were blocking all the exits. I had no choice. I threw up onto my plate.

It could have been the sauerkraut, and in fact some of it definitely *was* the sauerkraut, but the whole experience made me feel very alone. This was not what I had hoped pregnancy would be like. It was the first time that I really understood that A and I were different and that we had completely different priorities.

THINGS SETTLED DOWN again as soon as we got home, although I didn't forget the shock. I was frightened, happy, and desperate. And I threw up all day. I threw up for so many weeks and months that I thought there would be nothing left inside me, but the child stayed put. My belly grew and A touched it and said that he loved me. It was a blessing, a joy.

I didn't see the daily drudge coming at this point. Its arrival seemed impossible, as did the idea that we might stop loving each other. But the daily drudge found us. It found us and subjected us to all those loveless mornings when the oatmeal burned and the children wouldn't listen, when we couldn't look each other in the eye and just got on with the daily routine and longed to be without the other.

"Have you made Liva a sandwich?" I might ask.

"No, didn't you say you were going to do it?"

"I made Alva's packed lunch!"

"Well, couldn't you have made one for Liva, too, then?"

"I'm sure I could have, but I didn't think about it."

"Now I need to take everything out of the fridge again."

"Oh, what a shame!"

"I dressed them both, so you could at least have made their lunches."

And there you have it. The daily drudge: a balance sheet that's never equal.

IT'S STRANGE TO think about A and me as we were—as we will never be again. Our chance meeting in a bar, a moment I don't remember particularly well that has spawned three children. The encounter that changed my life is surprisingly vague in my memory. I remember that I was wearing a checked skirt. I remember that A was sitting on a bar stool and that he turned around when I came in. I remember thinking that it might have been chance, a coincidence that he turned around; maybe he heard the sound of the door opening or my friend Ruth's laugh. She laughed a lot, and she could have been laughing right then. Maybe she laughed as we came into the bar, and then A noticed me. Maybe he thought it was me laughing.

I went up to the bar and stood beside him. He asked me what I did. I gave some evasive, cocky answer. I don't remember what I was thinking as I stood there waiting for a drink. I didn't know what the future held for us. I would have stored it if I had: the thoughts, words, feelings, and pictures. I would have stored it and locked it away somewhere safe.

I T FEELS LIKE there's no oxygen left in the room. I open the door that goes out to the garden and take deep breaths of fresh air. I keep losing myself in the past and forgetting the task at hand. I have to come, but my hands are inactive. And so is Mr. Rabbit.

I pour myself a cup of lukewarm coffee from the thermos. Why should I feel more shame than anyone else? Is it my upbringing? My parents took me to church when I was little. I learned to be frightened of God above all. I can't remember thinking, at any point, of God as merciful. As a child I thought he would punish me if I did something bad — and I did lots of bad things. I waited for the punishment to be doled out. I often interpreted coincidences as punishment. I had stolen some chocolate from the cupboard, and then, soon after, the porcelain figurine that I loved the most fell off the shelf and smashed. God's punishment, I thought. I found a ten-kroner coin in Mom's bag that I stuffed in my pocket, and then an old wound on my knee tore open and left a nasty scar — God's punishment.

But more often, nothing happened, and God became more and more peripheral as I got older.

Am I ashamed because of God?

No, I don't believe in God anymore.

I google "masturbation in the Bible" and come across a really irritating blog written by an overly positive Christian woman. She's written a post about masturbating for the first time in her life: *The reason that I haven't tried before is not that I see it as a sin, but simply that it's not been necessary*, she says.

The lukewarm coffee gets stuck in my throat. The blogger says that she tried to find evidence in the Bible that states that masturbation is a sin and she hasn't found a single line. The closest she's got is the story of Onan, who had to marry his older brother's widow, an act that was custom in those days. It was thought to ensure the livelihood of the widow and the deceased's "descendants" because the first son would be seen as the brother's son. But Onan resisted and "spilled his seed on the ground" instead — hence the word *onanism*. We don't know whether he actually masturbated or just pulled out at the last moment, but whatever Onan did was evil in the eyes of God, it says.

I read the rest of the post, even though it makes me angry.

I tried once when my husband was out. I wanted to be more than ready for him when he did come home because I get more easily turned on when I'm aroused regularly ;-)

But I was so disappointed. Okay, I came, which was the point. I came several times, in fact. It was the first time I'd tried, so my expectations of the experience couldn't be too high, but I am after all a "well-trained wife" and I was disappointed that it was purely technique. There was no passion, no desire, no abandon, no loving touch, no sweaty embrace, and no unexpected caress. In fact, nothing of what really matters to me when I'm making love. It was a purely technical multiple orgasm.

It will be some time before I try it again.

What a hideously annoying woman. What can you say to something like that? I try to formulate a good comeback:

You write in your blog that masturbation is purely technique, without "sweaty embraces" and whatnot. I just wanted to say that I prefer to keep my multiple orgasms (which I have all the time) to myself, without the sweaty embraces and unexpected caresses.

— Multi-tasker

AND I had never really thought about getting married, but then we did all the same.

"I've booked the church," Mom said on the phone.

"What? The church?"

"Yes, if you're going to have a baby, you have to get married! I can't tell your grandparents about the baby until you're married."

"But he hasn't asked me, Mom! Are you totally crazy?"

"If he can get you pregnant, then he can marry you!"

"Mom, you're mad. How can I put—"

"The twenty-first of May," she said, and hung up the phone.

I tentatively broached the subject when A came home.

"Wouldn't it be fun to have a big party in the spring?"

"Parties are always fun."

I realized that I had to start from the other end.

"Do you love me?"

He gave me a puzzled look.

"Of course I love you. We're going to be a family. We're going to be together for the rest of our lives!"

Thank God. This was going better than I had expected.

"Well, why don't we sort of formalize it, then?"

"'Sort of formalize it?' What do you mean?"

"Maybe we could get married, or something like that."

"Or something like that," he parroted.

I took a deep breath before saying: "I think we should get married!"

A looked astonished, but smiled nonetheless.

"Is that a proposal?" he asked.

"Yes, you could call it that."

This wasn't going badly at all. Maybe he didn't have anything against getting married. Maybe I could pretend it was my idea.

"Darling, I want to share the rest of my life with you, but we don't need to get married to do that."

"Why not though?"

"We've got enough on our plates right now, including a baby on the way and apartment that needs to be readied."

Yes, these were fair arguments. I would have agreed if Mom hadn't booked the church.

"I don't want to live in sin," I burst out.

"Live in sin?"

"Yes. I want to be married when the baby's born."

"Aha. This is your mother's doing. Admit that it's your mother!"

"She's booked the church for the twenty-first of May," I whispered. "We have to get married."

He was angry now.

"I am not going to get married just because your mother has decided that we should!"

"It's not just Mom; it's me too. I like you. I love you. I really do!"

"But why do we have to get married now?"

"So that Mom can tell Grandma and Granddad about the baby," I said sheepishly.

"Can't she just tell them?"

I tried to explain that it wasn't like that in our family; you just didn't get pregnant before you were married.

"I will get married when I want to get married!" A shouted, and stormed out the door.

I went for a checkup with the really nice midwife at the medical centre. Nothing really happened at the checkups; I just had to be weighed and they measured my tummy. We listened to the heartbeats on an ultrasound machine. The midwife was the sort of woman you would want as your mother. She was kind and gentle; A came along to meet her this time. I could see that he liked her.

"Is everything okay then?" the midwife asked.

My first instinct was to say yes, but then when I thought about it, I realized that no, everything was not okay. My mother had booked the church for me to get married before my belly got too big, but I had no one to meet me at the end of the aisle.

"No," I replied. "Everything's not okay."

Then the tears came, quite a lot of them, too. In fact, I was sobbing. A started to stroke my back, but that just made me cry even more.

"Is something wrong?" the midwife asked.

"You can certainly say that," I sobbed.

"But what is it then?"

"He doesn't want to marry me!" I said, pointing at A.

"Is that true?" the midwife asked, giving him a stern look.

"Well, I haven't..."

"You know that you should give her all the support she needs?"

"I don't want to live in sin!" I wailed.

"It's not that I don't *want* to marry her!"

"Well, then what's the problem?" the midwife and I chorused.

"I don't want to get married just because my mother-in-law has decided we should."

"I see," the midwife said.

"She booked the church without even asking us. I'd

like to be the first person to know that I'm going to get married!"

"I understand perfectly," the midwife said kindly. "Mothers-in-law can be difficult, especially when they're going to be grandmothers. They have a tendency to take over."

"You can say that again!"

"But you're an adult now, and you're going to be a father. You have to think about what's best for your child. And what's best for your child is what is best for your girlfriend."

"Exactly," I sniffed.

The midwife leaned forward and took A by the hand.

"I think you should get married, but do it your own way, without the mother-in-law."

I looked at A with pleading eyes. He was about to give in.

"Okay," he said. "But nothing big, with just a couple of good friends at the town hall."

"Yes," I said, beaming. The midwife patted us both happily on the head. Then she said that I'd put on three kilos, which was rather a lot.

I GOOGLE SOME MORE. This time I leave out the Bible and just type "masturbation" in the search box. All sorts of things come up, but the links are mostly for blogs with questions from young girls wanting to know how to do it. Grown women don't ask about that sort of thing. We *know* the answers. But teenagers, on the other hand, write in to various forums to ask a variety of important inquiries. For example:

I need some masturbation tips!!!!

— *Girl, 14*

Girl, 14 gets a long detailed reply from a nurse who believes that coming is a human right. She writes that "masturbating is a way to explore and pamper your body, but can also be used to discover your sexual feelings for others. Masturbation is healthy because it strengthens your heart and circulation, increases your sex drive and reduces anxiety and depression, and stimulates happiness hormones, which has a positive effect on your immune system."

She says that it is quite normal for boys and girls to masturbate, and that it's okay to do it several times a day. "When it comes to masturbation, you need time to get to know your erogenous zones, your body's sexual responses, and to discover what you like best. Not everyone responds in the same way, so it is difficult to give a set recipe. Some like fast and hard masturbation, whereas others prefer gentle stimulation. Some like to touch other parts of their body at the same time, and others like to focus entirely on the clitoris."

This is all well and good, I think, but what about the fourteen-year-olds who don't want to masturbate either gently or fast and hard?

The nurse does give some good advice, though, that makes me think she's onto something essential. She believes that spending too much time and energy focusing on the orgasm itself might detract from the pleasure of masturbating: "You come more easily when you enjoy yourself and let your feelings go, without thinking that it *has* to happen. Your feelings take over when your body is relaxed and you are not as fixated on the final result."

Why is an orgasm so important to this fourteen-year-old? How does she know that she needs it?

I am quite clearly not in the target group, but have a greater need for help than any fourteen-year-old—she has her whole life in front of her, after all. As long as I keep the content relevant, why can't I write a little letter to the nurse?

Dear Nurse,

I am fifteen years old and I have never had an orgasm. All my friends have had one, but nothing happens for me. I have tried to have sex with boys and girls (I thought that maybe I was a lesbian, but I don't think so anymore). I got a vibrator with an orgasm guarantee from Condomania, but it's not working. I've been masturbating for almost a week straight with no results other than a potential repetitive strain injury in my right arm. I think that I'm normal, but every time I'm nearly there, I start to think "it has to happen now" and then it doesn't. Also, the vibrator makes me think of lawnmowers, which makes me think of my dad, which makes me think of my granddad (they're the ones who cut the lawn) and then I definitely can't come.

What should I do?

— Desperate Capricorn

YOU CAN SAY what you want about my mother, but she can put together a wedding in record time. She managed to get everyone at the church and organize a seated dinner for seventy-five guests at a hotel, seemingly out of nowhere. She invited great uncles and aunts, neighbours, and school friends, many of whom I'd forgotten existed.

I wore a fantastic dress, even though I had never really dreamed of being a white bride. In fact, I had never thought it necessary to get married at all, but there I was, wearing a white silk dress with a long train and a veil and carrying a bouquet of white orchids. My stomach, which had swelled quite a lot, was not visible in the dress. I felt more beautiful than I had ever felt before.

I progressed slowly down the aisle with my father holding my arm. A was standing at the altar in full evening dress. The suit belonged to an uncle on my mother's side. The jacket was a little short at the sleeves, but not by a lot. Through the veil, I could see how handsome he looked. Was he a little *too* handsome?

I thought of all the men I had known with wives and children—wives they were sick of and who didn't understand them and children they didn't understand. Suddenly I could see what would happen once we got married. I saw my future flash before me and it didn't look good. I saw A becoming more and more distant, and a baby that wouldn't stop crying. I would be exhausted and ugly, with nothing left for A. He wouldn't get enough sex, but would continue to look good, and would start to have sex with a nineteen-year-old editorial assistant at work.

I was getting angrier with each step. Suddenly I was storming up the aisle with my Dad forcefully holding me back.

I was fuming under my veil by the time I got the altar and threw a left hook right at the bridegroom. He fell to the floor with a thud, and I felt more than a little proud of myself. I had to show him who was in charge before it was too late.

"Have you lost your mind?" Dad hissed.

"He deserves it," I sobbed back.

I could hear people moving uncomfortably in the pews. A was still lying on the floor, knocked out by events rather than the punch.

"What have you done?" Dad asked A.

The priest looked like he didn't know what to say.

"I don't know," A replied. "I really don't know! I agreed to all of this against my will!"

The priest, Dad, and A were all staring at me, and the repercussions of my actions started to sink in.

"It's not so much what you've done," I stammered, "but what you might do after we're married," I explained.

None of the three men seemed to understand me, and I'm not sure that I entirely understood myself, but it felt right at the time. I heard Mom's footsteps approaching the altar. I could see that Dad was aware of the problem. We both looked at the priest and said "carry on" in unison.

A got up. I whispered to him that I would explain everything later. We answered yes to all the questions. Mom sat back down in her seat. At the reception, I read an excerpt from *What to Expect When You're Expecting* about the various hormones that wreak havoc with a pregnant woman's body and make her do things she wouldn't otherwise do.

A gave a lovely speech and finished by saying that I wasn't the only one who had hit the bull's eye. He meant the baby. We got married. We had children. We were what we were supposed to be.

MOST COUPLES WHO are married or live together have sex one to two times a week, according to *Dagbladet*, which means that A and I are not so far off the average. Our routine is often the same: we go to bed with an air of expectation. I have no idea where it comes from, but I do know how I react will have consequences, even though I haven't done anything to encourage it. It's been over a week since the last time we had sex, and he's allowed to try at the one-week mark. Once we go past a week things start to get difficult; we both know we can't continue without it, so a week is our kind of boundary. Sometimes it can go to eight or nine days. I can roll over, turn on the light, get out the book I'm reading, and pretend not to notice how long it's been. After all, one week is not *that* long. I've read about people in *Dagbladet* who go without it for two months, but they believe that's a sign that something's wrong.

So is one week bad, or not?

If we haven't done it for a while, things get tricky. The air seems to get a bit thicker. There's more pressure. And the more time that passes, the worse it gets. I try to think of it as housework: if you do a little regularly then things don't get out of hand. If you don't, things build up and it's impossible to know where to start.

Sometimes he's remarkably less insistent. Why is that? I look at his computer and bingo — he's been watching porn. Is it the same to him if he watches porn or has sex with me? It would seem so, but it *isn't* the same. Does he want our life to be more like a porn film? Should I watch more porn? I read an article about dirty sex in *Dagbladet* the other day and wondered if it's what he wants. According to the paper, Norwegian women also have sex secrets. A thinks I'm lying. He thinks my fantasies are not about him, which is why I can't talk about them, but it's not true. Maybe he's read *Dagbladet*. The article said that Norwegian women didn't even reveal their sex secrets to their closest friends, that they lied about how many sexual partners they'd had, that they were turned on by other men, that they dreamed about force and submission, and that they watched at least as much porn as men.

I certainly don't dream about force and submission. And I don't watch porn; it's too unrealistic. But I've also learned you should keep things fresh, so perhaps I should humour A and pretend that we live in a porn film. I could stand in the kitchen in my sexiest underwear and pretend that I need a plumber because something is wrong with the sink. I can just imagine it:

I call to tell the plumber about the problem and he promises to come straightaway. I obviously don't get dressed. Why would I do that? The plumber is undoubtedly very experienced, so I stay in my racy underwear while I wait. He comes faster than emergency services, and his overalls are open to his navel. He asks if I can show him the leak. I get down on all fours and point under the sink, where I've put a bucket so the water doesn't spread any further. The plumber is distracted by my ass and forgets to look at the leak.

"Yes, I can see that you need a new pipe," he says.

"Yes," I almost groan.

"Is it urgent?" the plumber asks.

"Yes, it's very wet," I tell him.

"Let's take a look then," the plumber says. To my great surprise — and pleasure — he lets his overalls fall to the floor. He's naked underneath.

He takes me so hard from behind that I can't help moaning. I come — and he comes — with a pressure that I would love to have in the taps. (No, stop thinking about practicalities! No practical thoughts allowed!) He waves his penis around the room like a garden hose and sprays semen all over the kitchen, which I have just cleaned. Does he think about who's going to clean up after him? The thought doesn't even enter his head. Typical men! They assume that everything just cleans itself! No, porn is not for me.

A never tidies up after himself. His socks lie piled beside the bed until I pick them up. He doesn't clear the table when he's finished eating and says that he'll do it once he's had a quick rest. He knows I'll have done it long before. And then he wants to have sex. Doesn't he understand that it's not easy to fuel your desire when your husband behaves like a kid?

Maybe I should think differently. Perhaps I need to meet someone new to have an orgasm. I could have an exciting affair. We could do it in washrooms and offices. He could lift me up onto his hips and drive me into the wall, like they do in films, or he could dramatically clear the kitchen countertop and spread me out on it. It would obviously have to be his kitchen counter because if it were mine, I would immediately start to think about who was going to clear the broken glass and leftovers. I'm certain I would be able to come if I had sex with a new person, because it's not really surprising that nothing happens when you're drowning in fish sticks and dirty socks, is it?

Studies have shown that most women who lose their sex drive in a monogamous relationship soon find it again when they get a new partner. So perhaps the solution is to find another man?

I want to call Mom and ask for her opinion. It might

help me relax, which is what I need to do to come. My mom and I have never talked about sex, but we're both adults. There's nothing to stop us from talking about it now, but I still don't do it. Maybe it's because I know exactly what she would say: "The grass isn't greener on the other side." She always says that.

"I've put up with your father for all these years, even though he's nothing to write home about. I've put up with him because I know that the grass is no greener on the other side. If I found myself a new man, it would only be a matter of time before he was sitting on the toilet with his nose buried in a newspaper, or falling asleep in front of the television with his mouth open, just like your father. So what's the point?"

Exactly. There is no point.

The only result would be financial hardship.

And what good is that to anyone?

I didn't organize a wedding for seventy-five people only for you to get divorced a few years later.

For better or for worse! That's what you promised.

That's what Mom would say.

So I don't call her, but I admit to myself that at least she has a point. As far as I'm concerned, the "grass is greener" mentality hasn't worked with anyone else either. So why would it suddenly work now? It's obviously not the man who's to blame for my problems. It's me.

I am the problem.

M Y ARM IS tired. I will soon unquestionably have a repetitive strain injury, but I'm not going anywhere until I've come. I am going to lie here until I manage to come, and have a repetitive strain injury. But maybe I should get some air first? A bit of air wouldn't do me any harm.

I decide to collect the sofa covers from the dry cleaner. I get dressed and make myself up as best I can. My lips are bright red. I try to look as ravenous as possible. The dry cleaning man will notice me, whether he wants to or not.

Ludmila looks at me. Martin is sitting in her arms, whining. I walk past casually.

HE'S NOT THERE. The dry cleaning man is not at work, and his wife is standing behind the counter, smiling, instead. I wait for as long as possible before handing over the receipt. She comes back with the covers wrapped in blue plastic.

"I'm afraid we couldn't manage to get them completely clean," she says apologetically.

"I see."

"Yes, it's not easy to get excrement off white fabric."

"Right," I say, and pay up.

I'M PERHAPS A little disappointed that the dry cleaning man wasn't there. But what did I think was going to happen? That we'd jump on each other in the back room?

I think about my *Miss Julie* project. It just seems more and more ridiculous. People want to read about reality and lived lives. There's no doubt that Strindberg is interesting, but he's a man: a man who thinks he's a woman, just like Gustave Flaubert.

"Madame Bovary, *c'est moi*," Flaubert said.

But he wasn't Emma. How could he be?

As I pass the coffee shop next door, I see the dry cleaning man sitting in the window reading *Nausea* by Sartre.

"Appropriate," I think.

REST DAY

I'M GOING OUT travelling. I'm only going to be away for one night, but that's longer than I've been out of Oslo alone for more than two years. I'm going to give a talk on creative writing to the editorial staff of a newspaper in Molde, and I'm dreading it. It's been a while since I've done anything like that. I'm scared that I haven't prepared enough, but nevertheless it's an enormous relief to be getting away. Ludmila has arranged to visit the family she used to work for, which makes me happy, because now A will see what my days are really like.

It can't be that hard to look after your own children? At least, that's what A says when I complain.

I feel triumphant as I stand by the door with my suitcase. Now A will see; he'll see what it's like to be awake every hour throughout the night, to never be able to sit in peace for more than ten minutes, and to constantly have vomit and food on your clothes.

I'm packed and ready to go. When the doorbell rings, I have no idea who it might be.

Mom is standing outside. She's got a rather large suitcase with her and is wearing a coat that I've never seen before. She looks as though she's been crying.

"I've left your father," she says.

I don't know what to say. I could never have imagined this, not even in my wildest dreams.

"Why?" I ask.

"Isn't that obvious?"

I think so hard you can hear my brain creaking.

"No."

"He only ever thinks of himself, fishing, and cards!"

This is news to me.

"What about the grass never being greener on the other side?"

"At my age there is no other side. I want to have some peace and quiet. I want to be on my own. I want to go to the Mediterranean. Your father doesn't add anything to my life anyway, so there is absolutely no reason for him to continue being part of it."

"But where are you going to live?"

Mom looks at her suitcase before raising her eyebrows.

"I thought that perhaps I could stay here... for a while. Until I find my own place?"

For a moment, I feel the panic rising. I've got my hands full with my own problems. I can't even have an orgasm, and now my mother wants to move in.

"There's not enough room. You know that."

"Oh yes, of course, you've got *her*. You would choose her over me."

"Yes, and you chose Dad. You chose to live with Dad!"

"But I could sleep on the sofa, couldn't I? Just for a few days. Don't you think that would be okay?"

"Now is not a good time, Mom. I'm going away."

I push my small suitcase in front of her somewhat bigger suitcase to emphasize this point.

"Don't you think A and the children might need me when you're not here? I could bake. The children love it when I bake."

I begrudge any help that A might get when I am finally away. Half the point is that he can see what it's like to be alone with the children.

"It's not a good time, Mom. Like I said, I'm away for work and we…"

"So you're serious? You would turn away your own mother?"

"Yes."

I push her to one side and lock the door.

THE TALK IN Molde goes well — not brilliantly — but well. After the seminar, I go out to eat with some of the journalists. They speak quickly and furiously about things I know nothing about. I feel left out, and it's been a long time since I felt that way. I've only read interior decorating magazines and *Elle* in the past year. I can't follow the conversation. I could have talked about masturbation or female orgasms, since I know quite a lot about them now, but fortunately I decide that it might send the wrong signals.

I begin to say silly things after a few glasses of wine. The man sitting next to me laughs. I say more silly things and the journalist laughs even more. The others leave and eventually it's just the two of us left. He tells me that he was the person who arranged for me to come and speak. He's read all my books and is a big fan. He puts a hand on my thigh while he's saying it. What does he think?

A few years ago, I would have shouted at him. *Who do you think you are?*

But instead I get up and go to the toilet. I look at my face in the mirror and go up to my hotel room, three floors above the restaurant. My mother has tried to call me six times. A has not tried to contact me, which is surprising.

I phone Mom and apologize.

"Sorry, I'm not myself at the moment."

"But this isn't about you. It's about me and your father."

"I know, but you've always said that the grass isn't greener. You've always said that perseverance is the only thing that matters."

"I know that I've said that in the past—I believed it. But now I'm not so sure."

I hear a man's voice in the background. My mother stifles a giggle.

"Where are you? I just think I was a bit harsh. Of course you can stay on the sofa. The covers have just been cleaned."

"That's very sweet of you, darling, but I don't want to intrude. You've got enough on your plate right now. I understand."

The man's voice calls again. More giggling.

"I have to go. Speak again soon. I'll be staying in town."

Mom hangs up. She's found out that the grass is greener on the other side. I feel sick.

I WAKE UP at six o'clock and it's impossible to get back to sleep. I put on a white suit that I bought in a moment of bravado. It was far too expensive, but it fits perfectly. And it contrasts well with my dark hair. It's the kind of suit that A will like, so I'm sure he'll forgive the extravagance. A is quite generous. When I buy something, he seldom protests. He thinks I deserve it. I'm so glad that I went to bed last night.

Outside, the Romsdal Alps rise up sharply against the blue sky. I go to have breakfast alone and feel good in my white suit. For the first few minutes I take great pleasure in an egg that is boiled to perfection for once, as well as the beautifully sliced bread and smoked salmon. The dining room is almost empty. Three men in suits are having an animated conversation two tables away. They don't notice me. I read the papers that were lying so invitingly on a table in the corner. This is what I have wanted for a long time: peace, salmon, papers. I really try to enjoy it, but I miss my children: their hands, enthusiasm, and demands, and how things were before Ludmila came. I am immensely irritated with myself. Why can't I just enjoy the moment, like A can?

The men at the table have still not even looked in

my direction. They probably would have five years ago. Perhaps the white suit isn't so nice after all; or rather, it's just not "me." I regret buying it.

I get a text from Vibeke right before I board the plane. I haven't heard from her since what I have come to think of as *the episode*. She's texting me to say that she's taken the pillows in for dry cleaning and will send me the bill. My first thought is that it's too late to send them to my dry cleaning man, but I realize that it's a stupid thought.

I CAN FEEL THE anticipation in my body as I put the key in the lock. Now A will know how important I am for the family and that I keep everything together. He'll know that he and the children would never manage without me.

I hear Alva's bubbling laughter. They're lying on the living room floor—on the clean living room floor. Alva is jumping on A. Martin is standing on the floor beside them waving his hands around. The room smells of soap. There are two empty pizza boxes on the dining table. The three of them don't even hear me coming.

"Boo," I say.

Silence descends upon the room. Martin lights up and runs towards me. Alva pretends she's offended and continues to jump on A.

"Have you washed the floor?"

"Yes," A says, proudly.

"You know you shouldn't use soap on parquet."

"Is that such a big deal?"

"Yes, it is a big deal. It's not good, since the floors aren't oiled. We've been living here for two years now, and you still haven't oiled the floors. So soap is not a good idea."

The words just pour out.

I could so easily have been more positive and started by thanking him for taking the time to clean the house. I could have thrown myself into the game and into A's arms. I could have said nice things, but I don't. I need to tell him what's wrong.

If he can be on his own with the kids and can clean the house and still be in a good mood, then what can I do? What makes me indispensible?

I shrug and look at the pizza boxes on the table.

"That's not very healthy, is it?"

"Is that such a big deal?" he says again, this time his voice slightly sharper than before.

The children pick up on the tone and the change in atmosphere. They stop laughing. Martin pulls himself loose and starts to play with the building blocks in his toy corner. Alva goes into her room silently to find the pacifier that she can't live without. A turns on the television.

"It was good of you to clean," I say.

Ludmila is back in place the next day.

ONCE I'M ENSCONCED back in bed again, I look through the copies of *Dagbladet* that are piled up beside me. I study Atle Jansen's byline picture. I decide to call him. He's the one who's made me believe there's something wrong with me. If it hadn't been for Atle Jansen, I might never have decided to lie down here full-time. If it hadn't been for Atle Jansen, I might never have felt like a failure.

I feel myself getting angry just thinking about him. I'm going to give him a piece of my mind! Of course I could write him an email (the address is under the byline picture on all his articles about orgasms), but I don't feel it's enough to write. I want to talk to — preferably scream at — Atle Jansen. What I'm going to scream, I'm not sure, but it will be loud and it will be brutal.

I find his number on the Internet. It rings and rings and then finally he answers.

"Hello," says a voice that is presumably Atle Jansen. His voice is just as jovial as I imagined it would be.

"You bastard," I hiss into the receiver.

"I'm sorry?" he stammers.

"Why are you writing all this crap about orgasms? Are you not a grown man? Do you not have better things to do with your time?"

I tell him what a failure I feel like in the wake of reading all his articles; I tell him that I have *never* had an orgasm. It's possible that I'm angrier than I need be.

"I'm just doing my job," Atle Jansen says. I can tell that he's a bit put out.

But surprisingly, Atle Jansen does not go on the defensive. It's possible that other people have phoned him. He tries to explain himself as best he can. If I had done my research, I would know that he doesn't only write about orgasms. On the contrary, he has also written a long series of articles about oil workers in the North Sea, which was interesting. He doesn't find all this orgasm crap stimulating.

"No, it's not," I say, and then I tell him that I know he got the SKUP Award in 2007.

Atle Jansen explains that it's the editors who get him to do it. It's one of the consequences of the death of the newspaper, he says. If there's no sex, people won't buy it. Sadly, that's just the way things are. Atle Jansen's problem is that he's worried he'll be remembered as the man who wrote about orgasms in *Dagbladet*, but it's his articles on the oil workers that he *wants* to be remembered for.

"Do you promise to stop then?"

"Unfortunately, I can't promise anything," he says, but I can hear that he's taking me seriously, and that's not so bad in itself.

"If I don't write about it, they'll just get someone else to write about it instead," he says.

"I know," I reply.

And then we end the conversation. I've decided that I like Atle Jansen and that it's possible he has qualities that the world has not yet recognized.

DAY 7

THE DAY STARTS perfectly. Ludmila has probably slept in, which suits me fine. I'm alone with Martin in the kitchen. We have a nice breakfast with hot chocolate and warm rolls. Martin babbles away. I enjoy every second. What made me want an au pair so badly?

I suddenly realize that I used to enjoy the mornings. I liked the peace that finally descended throughout the house once all the others had left and Martin took his morning nap. I enjoyed the quiet and the coffee.

There's no room in the kitchen for anyone other than me, but now Ludmila's here, and every morning she marches over to the kettle as though it was her kettle. She drinks that green, slimy concoction that I still haven't managed to identify and clogs the drain with her green sludge. It smells suspect. And so does her perfume. It makes me retch. I lie on the bed and hope that she'll disappear or go do something or take her language course soon. Then Martin wakes up and I feel reluctant to give him to her, but I have to. It wouldn't look good otherwise. Why would I need an au pair if she's not going to look after my child?

A has left for work. He leaves earlier now, with a far clearer conscience than before. He thinks everything's hunky dory at home and I can't tell him that it's not, because then I would sound difficult and unreasonable. I was the one who wanted an au pair.

I can hear Ludmila in the bathroom and know that she'll come in any minute now to use the kettle. I leaf manically through *Aftenposten*. Is there anything to do? Anywhere I can go? Toddler Time at the movie theatre? No, I can't go to Toddler Time without Martin, and I can't take Martin with me, because then A will probably hear about it and ask why I'm not working.

Is having an au pair in general the problem, or is it something about Ludmila in particular? Like I said, her perfume is hideous. It makes me want to throw up. And there's Michael, who hangs around smirking. And then there's all the sighing. The sighs are perhaps the worst. She sighs when she puts a plate in the dishwasher, she sighs when she takes it out. She sighs when she picks Martin up from the floor. Is that really necessary?

A friend of mine says that sighing is typical for people from Eastern Europe.

"It's a bit like Asians," she says.

"What do you mean?"

"Asians always smile, don't they? We think that everyone from the Philippines is happy because they're always smiling, but maybe they're not."

"Right?"

"So it's probably not the case that everyone from Eastern Europe is depressed all the time, just because they sigh."

Ludmila comes in and starts her brewing. I suggest that she take Martin out to the park. Her Norwegian course starts in a couple of hours. If she goes now, then I won't have to see her for a while. She shrugs, picks up Martin, sighs, and struggles to get him into his winter snowsuit. He cries and wants me to come.

"Maybe it's best if you leave," Ludmila says.

I nod and creep back down to the bedroom, take a deep breath, and pull out the vibrator. The sight of it does not fill me with pleasure. I might as well give up.

LUDMILA HAS GONE to her Norwegian class. She won't be back for a few hours. I rock Martin's stroller impatiently, as if I can't get rid of him soon enough, and act like I've got something important to do. I'm looking forward to his falling asleep so I can go back into the house and be alone.

I leave the door ajar so he doesn't wake up again,

tiptoe in, and finally let my shoulders drop when there are no protests from outside. There are some cups and plates by the sink, so I put them in the dishwasher and wipe the countertop with a damp cloth. Maybe it's because I'm humming, but I certainly don't notice Michael until he's breathing down my neck and has put a dirty hand around my waist. I'm startled and react with anger.

"Shh," Michael says.

He smells like beer.

"Ludmila's not here," I say hastily.

"So?" He gives a rather exaggerated shrug.

I can feel my vagina pounding, and I think his breath is causing it. I back away, but he grabs my waist again. There's no force in his arm. It touches me lightly, but his arm feels heavy. Jean, I think. He's Jean.

His dirty hands move up and slide over my breasts that I thought couldn't register anything other than babies' mouths, but they harden under his rough hands. My body slowly starts to open. If he moved his hands down he'd discover that everything was wet. I want him to feel it; I want his hand to move down because then I wouldn't need to answer whether I want it or not. My body will answer for me. The gravity in my vagina makes my knees wobble. *He* has an orgasm guarantee, I think, as his hand moves slowly, far too slowly, down.

At first, I don't register the feeble crying because I feel

like it has nothing to do with me. Then slowly it dawns on me that it's Martin who's crying.

I push Michael away and storm towards the door. My cheeks are burning, and every fibre in my body is pulsing. Michael is still in the house. I pick Martin up and hold him to me. I could have come, I think. If things had been allowed to follow their course, I could have come.

Next door, Camilla comes out to collect the mail.

"It's a little chilly today," she says and shivers.

"Yes," I reply, but I'm burning.

I GO FOR a long walk with Martin. I walk so that my body will calm down and my heart won't pound any faster than the pace that I'm walking. The heart is a practical muscle; it has to think of the most important things first, so I walk at a furious pace, pushing the stroller in front of me until my mouth tastes of metal.

When we get home, Martin is asleep, even though he shouldn't be. Ludmila is presumably in the house working. I'm on my way over to the fridge to look for a cucumber or carrot to give something organic a last chance, when I see Michael's shoes in the hall. They're dirty and dusty work shoes that have been thrown into a corner. The dirt has fallen off and scattered on Martin's winter snowsuit. I hear sounds from Ludmila's room. Ludmila is moaning and crying out. Michael is crying out. I stand in the doorway and imagine Michael's amber eyes rolling back into his head when he comes and cries out, how his dirty working hands are holding on to Ludmila.

I start to tidy. Ludmila has obviously not done what she should have. I take off my coat and make a lot of noise putting some cups into the dishwasher. Ludmila comes rushing out of the room.

"I didn't hear you coming," she says, apologetically.

"I wish I could say the same thing."

"Huh?" Ludmila looks at me, disconcerted.

"You have a visitor?"

She says nothing. I try to give her a stern look.

"Michael came to sort out the TV channels."

"But you don't watch TV, Ludmila."

"I do, a bit. Sometimes I do."

"Did he sort it out then?"

She nods and pushes me to one side and puts the rest of the cups in the dishwasher.

Michael comes out of the room as well. He winks. I don't know whether he's winking at Ludmila or me. Maybe it's some kind of strategy. Do I see Michael as Jean? If that's the case, Ludmila is Kristine. No, that doesn't work. Nothing works.

I CALL A at work and tell him what's happened: Ludmila was shamelessly having sex with Michael when she was supposed to be working.

"She has every right to have a sex life. God knows, not everyone in the house does!"

"Great, so now you've had your dig! I've got nothing against Ludmila having sex, only that she does it when she's supposed to be working and looking after *your* child!"

"I thought Martin was with you?"

"Yes, so she was supposed to be doing the housework then!"

A has been fooled because she makes good food and very good cabbage rolls. It doesn't take much to win him over; he's one of the best examples of food being the way to a man's heart.

"Fine. I'll tell her she can just carry on sleeping with Polish labourers when she's supposed to be working."

"Do that," A says.

I slam down the phone. Ludmila is clearly a nymphomaniac, I think. What if she hits on A? Perhaps she already has? Maybe there's more than cabbage rolls behind his good-natured, tolerant tone?

I know that it's nonsense—A wouldn't do that—and Ludmila isn't a nymphomaniac. I don't even really know the definition of a nymphomaniac. I know there's something called Persistent Genital Arousal Disorder that is a rare condition, which according to Wikipedia results in a "spontaneous, persistent, and uncontrollable genital arousal, with or without orgasm or genital engorgement, unrelated to any feelings of sexual desire." It's quite a terrible illness. Women who suffer from it are constantly horny; they masturbate until they draw blood and they can't talk to anyone about it, because they're both embarrassed and afraid they won't be taken seriously. Most of them end up completely isolating themselves. Having read about women who have to live with this syndrome, I should just be glad that all I have to deal with is the fact that I can't come. But is not having an orgasm also an illness?

THE PHARMACEUTICAL INDUSTRY in the U.S. has called the inability to come "sexual dysfunction disorder." They've devised a term so they can profit off the drugs they sell for the condition. Companies are pouring enormous resources into discovering new types of treatments they can monetize that will cure the grave condition of "sexual dysfunction disorder" — Viagra for women, as one example. The company that owns the patents for the pill that makes women horny will undoubtedly get rich, but these people haven't thought about the pill's potential consequences. The world will probably not function as well if women are as horny as men and willing to do almost anything to get a lay. Will we reconsider the societal expectations of female sexuality? After all, women are only supposed to be suitably horny, not *too* horny, because that's vulgar and shameful, in the same way that it's shameful not to be horny.

So pharmaceutical companies should really think about the big picture before they start mass-producing pills that create sexed-up women.

THERE WAS NOT only a flasher in the town where I grew up, but also a nymphomaniac. At least, that's what everyone called her. She was a tall, lanky creature who wandered the streets in a far-too-short skirt. There was something evasive and doe-like about her eyes, as though she knew what people said behind her back. I didn't know her — nobody did. We only knew that she was a nymphomaniac. Someone, who no one knew personally, had seen her running naked through the woods in search of men. The boys in my class said that she had a cunt that was as deep as a foxhole and that she could never get enough cock. No one knew her name. We simply dubbed her "the nymphomaniac." Whenever we said the words, everyone knew who we were talking about. Her lovers were mostly foreigners who worked in the shipyard. We excused them because they couldn't possibly know who she was, and as one of the boys said, "She doesn't look that bad." He wouldn't have minded a go himself, if only she wasn't a nymphomaniac.

She disappeared. I didn't think about it until many years later, when I was sitting on the train on the way home to visit my parents. The nymphomaniac was sitting across from me with a crying baby on her lap, and a three- or four-year-old boy in the seat beside her. She was wearing a black blazer and jeans. She had red cheeks and still looked young. She got up and bounced the baby as she walked up and down the aisle, humming quietly. She had lost her doe-like, evasive appearance, which would have seemed out of place with her current situation. Her little, fair-haired boy followed her around the train, whining. Her baby wouldn't stop crying. It struck me that no one else on the train would have dreamed of calling her a nymphomaniac. The children had normalized her and made her less of a target than

I T'S ONLY LATER that evening that the relief hits me: relief that nothing happened with Michael. I look at the children and at A; I look at Ludmila and think of the noises she made in her bedroom with Michael; I think about what Michael might have done with her. And I feel only relief.

What has the episode with Michael taught me? I need to allow myself to be caught up in the moment and be spontaneous. Lawnmowers have to be kept out of it, but that's easier said than done when I'm trying to make *it* happen.

"Julie, don't think about lawnmowers!" I say to myself while I'm lying in bed.

The sky is dark and a cold blue. A must have put the children to bed. I hear his footsteps up in the kitchen, then coming down the stairs, and then standing outside the door, hesitating.

"Julie, what are you doing in there?"

"Nothing," I respond.

"You've been in there all day. Is the migraine any better?"

"Don't know."

"Well, I just wanted to let you know that I was hoping to go to bed soon."

"You can sleep on the sofa. The covers have been cleaned."

"I'd like my book, please."

"Okay, just go upstairs and sort out the sofa."

I hear his resigned footsteps go back up the stairs. I throw his Solstad novel out the door, which I then lock again. I hear him and Ludmila talking about something. They laugh and I realize it's becoming more and more unbearable to have her around. She is clearly a nymphomaniac. I can't stop imagining her face, how it twists in ecstasy when Michael penetrates her, and I feel deep revulsion each time.

My own inadequacy overpowers me. I don't want to see Ludmila's face, but I can't get the image out of my head.

"She looks after your child," I say to myself.

I consider that this could be the reason why I'm so aggressive and far too critical of anything she does.

"Why do you do it like *that* and not like *this*?"

She has certainly has a sharp tongue and always finds a way to defend herself. As a rule, she explains that the way she's doing it is how it's done in Ukraine. In fact, she starts an astonishing number of sentences with "in Ukraine."

Once, she measured her temperature when she was sick in bed. It was 36.9.

"Oh, thankfully you don't have a fever then," I said.

"In Ukraine, 36.9 is fever," she said.

"No, 36.9 is not a fever in any country," I replied.

"It is," she retorted.

I regret not choosing the cardiologist. It would probably have worked out better.

I would be able to talk to the cardiologist. I could have taught her Norwegian and she could have kept me updated on the most recent heart research.

It is now my indisputable right to return Mr. Rabbit back to where he came from. It is my indisputable right to push him over the counter, look the girl from northern Norway in the eye and say: "It didn't work. And no one can say I didn't try. Money back, please!"

A KIND OF
SUCCESS

I PUT MY hand into the mailbox. At first I don't realize what is about to happen when I pull out an envelope from the Oslo Council. I open it indifferently and look down with limited interest at the contents. Suddenly the impact of the words dawns on me: we've got a spot in preschool.

We're free!

We can ask Ludmila to leave!

"I'm sorry," I will say. "That's just the way things go."

Everything will return to the way it was before. The kitchen will once again belong to me and no one else. I can get my office back. I'll start using the sofa with the purple cushions. I won't have to deal with the perfume, the nausea, the sound of the kettle, or Michael's mocking eyes. I will get my life back.

Finally it's over. We've got a spot—a full-time spot.

I'll wait a bit to tell her. I'll explain that there's nothing I can do. *We have to think about what's best*

*for Martin, and we can't afford to keep you and pay for
preschool.*

I play through the scene in my head, but Ludmila
appears before I'm actually ready.

Her face goes red when I explain the situation.

"Couldn't I just stay here until college starts?"

I can see that she's stressed. And it makes me happy.

"No, I'm afraid you can't stay here until college starts.
Martin needs the room. He's too big to be sleeping in
our room now. I'm sure you understand."

"In Ukrai—"

"No," I interrupt.

Her lips begin to tremble and her eyes fill up with
tears. I just want to be rid of her—to get her out. I know
there's no rush with Martin, but I close my eyes, take
a deep breath, and tell Ludmila that it's not possible. I
say no to her cabbage rolls, to the visits from Michael,
and to the smell of spices and perfume.

"You'll have to move out on the weekend. That's just
the way things go," I say.

THE NURSE HAS sent me an answer:

Dear Capricorn,

You are only fifteen, so don't get too fixated on the fact that you haven't managed to have an orgasm so far. In the course of your life, you will meet lots of boys and experience many things. The orgasm will come if you just stop focusing on it so much.

Good luck!

— The Nurse

M Y RIGHT ARM aches. The orgasm guarantee has run out. I feel relieved. I don't need to go into Condomania and say that I want my money back; I don't need to hear the girl from northern Norway with the lips tell me that she thought it was impossible for me not to come with Mr. Rabbit. It's too late. The thought is comforting and it makes it easier to fail.

I carry on masturbating with renewed energy. I don't *need* to do it, but I continue because I want to — I actually feel that something is happening. It starts down in my legs, an unbearable tickle that rises up towards the centre. It's going to happen, I can feel it — it's going to happen! I close my eyes and I don't think about lawn-mowers. The sound of Mr. Rabbit has become a part of my body's rhythm. I wait for the orgasm that's on its way and prepare myself to let loose a primal scream. But then I notice that Mr. Rabbit is slowing down like he can't take it anymore. Does he think there have been too many obstacles in our relationship and that enough is enough? Is this really happening?

Yes.

The batteries have run out.

I have to get new batteries, and fast. I can't find any in the kitchen. It's not that long since I bought some, because Martin has so many laser swords and cars. I take one of his fire trucks from the shelf and try to open the little battery chamber, which of course requires a small screwdriver. The toolbox is in the shed and the moment will be gone by the time I get dressed to go out there. I go back to my bed and carry on manually, but I've already started to think about the location of the screwdriver, and when I last used it. As soon as you start thinking practical thoughts, it's too late. I've learned that much.

I sigh, get up from the bed and stand the vibrator at the back of Martin's toy shelf.

Mr. Rabbit and I have had enough. We've given up.

Do I feel defeated or just relieved?

Is it really a problem for *me* that I'm not horny — that I can't come — and could have a disorder of sorts?

No, it isn't, in fact. It's a problem for A: not physically, of course, but as long as I don't come, he'll think there's something wrong with him as a man. Our relationship will become imbalanced if he thinks he's inadequate as a man and undesirable. An imbalance that could lead to depression or divorce — and I don't want either. I want to be happy. Is that too much to ask?

I know what I have to do.

I go into the living room where A is sleeping. He barely opens his eyes. I straddle him.

"I've done it," I whisper in his ear.

"Done what?"

He's not quite awake yet.

"I've managed to have an orgasm."

Now he's completely awake.

"So that's what you've been doing? But how and why?"

"Shhh," I whisper and start to move slowly on top of him.

A presses his finger against my clitoris, a little too hard. I moan.

"Yes," I whisper.

He slides into me, moves deftly in and out as he frantically massages my breasts.

He lies back and closes his eyes. I think about Ludmila and that fact that I'm rid of her. I will soon have my home back and can reclaim the room with the purple cushions.

My vagina aches, but I fake the perfect orgasm. I think about Ludmila and fake the perfect orgasm. I've missed faking. I've missed being able to give A something to make him happy in that way. It's over pretty quickly. A reaches his usual point of ecstasy and comes all over the freshly dry cleaned sofa covers.

"Was that necessary?" I ask.

"What did you say?"

"Nothing, just go back to sleep."

"Was it good?"

I nod.

"I'm so happy for you," A says. "Really happy."

"Sleep," I say, and kiss him on the check. Then I pull the blanket over him.

"I can't believe you just commented on the sofa," he mutters with a contented sigh.

I hear the stairs creak hesitantly and recognize Alva's small padding feet. Her voice fumbles in the dark.

"Mommy, I can't sleep!"

"You can't sleep?"

"No, I keep dreaming there's a horrible witch who wants to cut my head off."

"There, there," I say and pull her tiny body to mine. "There's no witch, you know that."

"Can you come, Mommy?"

Her shiny childish eyes plead with me.

"Of course I can," I say, as I carry her back up the stairs.

I hear A snoring lightly behind me.

© Fredrik Arff

SELMA LØNNING AARØ IS a newspaper columnist for *Dagbladet* and *Klassekampen* in Norway. Her first novel, *The Final Story*, won the Cappelen Prize for Best Debut Novel in 1995, and is the imaginative tale of a young woman's erotic adventures. She has since written six novels for adults and two books for children. Her work has been translated into five languages. She lives in Oslo.

KARI DICKSON WAS born in Edinburgh, Scotland, and grew up bilingually — her mother is Norwegian and her grandparents could not speak English. She has a B.A. in Scandinavian studies and an M.A. in translation. She has translated works by Roslund & Hellström, Anne Holt, Henrik Ibsen, and Stein Erik Lunde & Øyvind Torseter. She lives in Edinburgh.